AF424397

Infernal Tramps: Tales of Weird Terror by Alex Grass
First Edition 2026

HORROR/FICTION

ISBN 978-1-7358885-6-9
(eBook) 978-1-7358885-7-6
Library of Congress Control Number 2026911966

DICKINSON PUBLISHING GROUP
Brooklyn | Delaware

INQUIRIES AND CORRESPONDENCE:
yokhanan.zevi@dickinsonpublishinggroup.com

No generative artificial intelligence (AI) was used to write this book. The author expressly prohibits the use of his work in conjunction with AI.

INFERNAL TRAMPS

TALES OF WEIRD TERROR

BY ALEX GRASS

THE STORIES

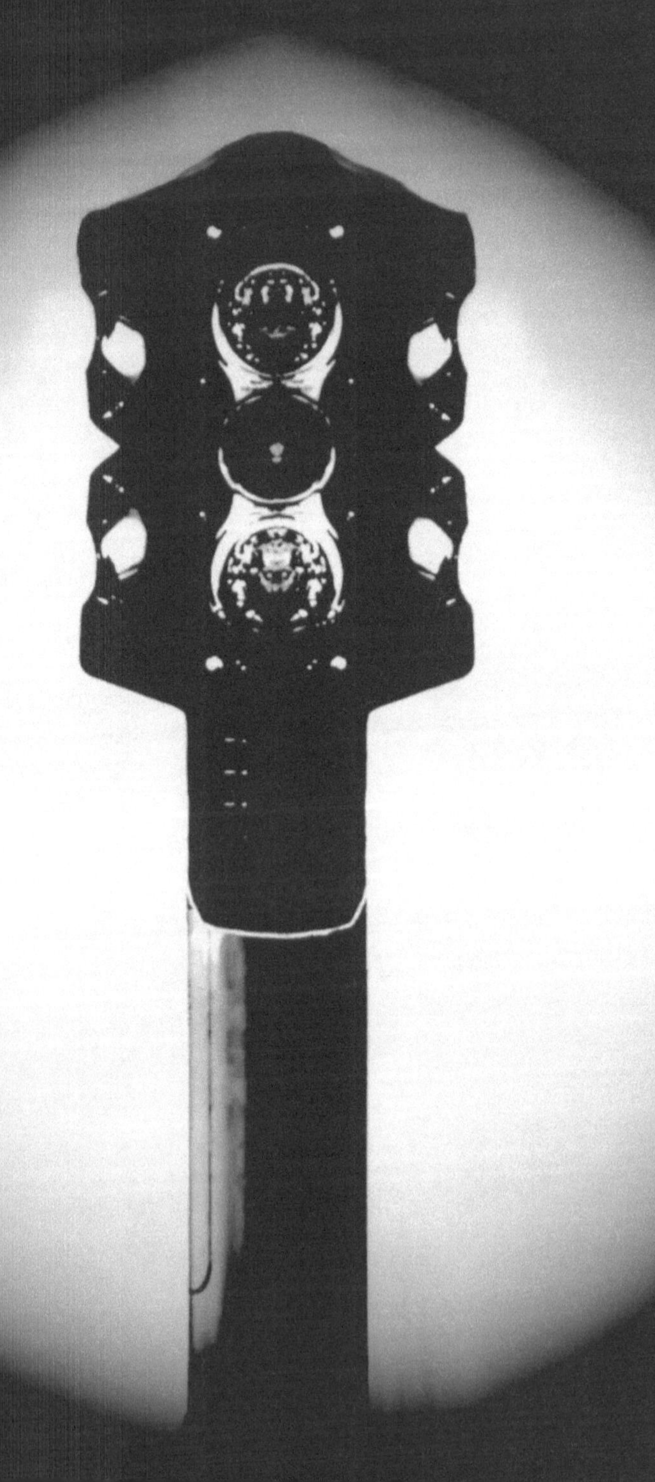

THE TEZCAT APPARATUS

The device that the salesman had out on the coffee table in Samarium's living room looked like someone had taken the mechanical movement from the guts of a music box and drilled it sideways into a miniature model of an old-fashioned phone booth. An LCD screen was mounted to the exterior housing.

"How does it keep birds and critters out of the garden?" Samarium asked.

The grandfatherly salesman wore a curious wardrobe; filthy sneakers and a Nehru suit, with black sunglasses too small to conceal his cataracted eyes. There was a glove on his right hand, with the two middle sheaths sewn shut where those fingers were missing.

"It's a combination of sonic deterrence and pattern recognition. If the animal doesn't bother with what you're growing, the Tezcat Apparatus will leave the animal alone. But if the animal goes nosing in your furrows, the Apparatus will deter them from doing it again. Even an animal won't trade its life for a single carrot."

"It looks expensive," Samarium said, reaching toward the brassy gold hardware along the hinges. He was drawn to glittering appurtenance in the way of a magpie.

"Please don't touch that," the salesman said. He wasn't looking at Samarium or the Apparatus and, by all appearances, was almost certainly blind. "Premature physical contact with the Apparatus is not recommended."

"Why? Is it dangerous?"

The salesman visibly restrained himself from frowning. "No, but it is a sensitive device. It's been carefully calibrated. The Apparatus is a model of mechanical and computational durability. But fiddling with it before placement affects its pattern recognition. It's best not to touch until it's been mounted and activated."

"Does it work?"

"Most assuredly, sir," the salesman said. "Our other test customers have reported a one-hundred percent reduction in invasive destruction. Most have elected to keep the Apparatus in place after the trial period."

"Test customers?"

"Yes, sir. I should have been clearer. You see, the Tezcat Apparatus is not readily available for purchase by the public. You have been selected as one of the domiciliary testing sites. If you're interested, of course."

Samarium clicked his teeth with his tongue. He took a sip of his coffee. "Well, I'd sure like to keep those goddamn ground squirrels and jackrabbits out of my root veggies," he said. "How much does it cost?"

The salesman knowingly smiled. "We provide it to you at no cost. Maintenance and repairs are free. We just ask to be able to regularly check the Apparatus so we can make updates and log functionality. To improve the product before it's available to the public-at-large."

"Free, huh?" Samarium smiled.

"Yes, sir."

"Can't get no better than that."

The salesman grinned. "No, sir, you cannot."

"Shit," Samarium said, "I'll take it."

———

SAMARIUM SIPPED HIS MORNING COFFEE AS HE WATCHED A jackrabbit lope around his patch of rutabagas. He kept looking back and forth between the Apparatus mounted on the wood pole and the jackrabbit sniffing at his plantings.

"Goddamnit," he said in a grumbling complaint, "do something."

An array of green dots abruptly projected from the Apparatus and swept over the jackrabbit. As the jackrabbit stumbled and rolled onto its back, Samarium, caught by surprise, twitched a little bit and tucked his chin into his neck.

He went outside and sized up the varmint, nudging it with the toe of his shoe. The jackrabbit leapt up, startling Samarium back so he spilled coffee on himself. "Shit!" Then the fleet-footed hare took flight, bounding toward a wooded refuge of copse and bramble.

———

THE SAME THING HAPPENED A FEW DOZEN MORE TIMES—AT least, that was the frequency with which Samarium witnessed, firsthand, the Apparatus bathe the bushy-tailed intruders in a shower of neon green light.

At the end of the week, Samarium's doorbell rang. He'd quite conveniently scheduled the technician's visit on the Tezcat app and was expecting that visit presently.

He opened the door, and there was the old blind man in the Nehru suit and begrimed sneakers. The salesman-now-turned-tech held a large, empty duffel bag in one hand and a tablet in the other.

"Oh. It's you."

"Yes, it's me," the salesman said, smiling. "Is it alright if I go around back and run diagnostics?"

"Sure, sure, go ahead. You need me for anything?"

The salesman shook his head. "No, no, sir. Everything's well in hand."

Samarium settled in next to his kitchen window and watched the salesman enter his backyard. The salesman took out a touchscreen tablet and plugged it into the Tezcat Apparatus. Samarium squinted his eyes to narrow in on the Apparatus's LCD display directly facing his window. He saw computerized images of jackrabbits, squirrels, voles, coons, skunks and chipmunks run across the screen in sequence.

He watched as a group of living wild animals, in a correspondingly exact species ratio as in the on-screen sequence, gathered around the salesman. The salesman pressed a button on his tablet. All at once, the varmints all keeled over, paws pointed heavenward. All of them, to a one, all surely dead.

The salesman walked around, picking up the dozens of dead animals and stuffing them in his duffel bag. It took him five minutes to finish cleaning up the carcasses, at which point he departed Samarium's backyard.

The doorbell rang again. Samarium went to go answer. The salesman was pulling off his right glove as Samarium opened the door. The salesman was no longer missing his ring and middle finger.

"Alright, sir, that's it for the week," the man said as he took his sunglasses off his face and tucked them in his suit's outbreast pocket. His eyes were perfectly clear, absent any evidence there had ever been cataracts. "Just one last thing."

"Yes?" Samarium said.

"Would you be interested in trying out our new home security system?"

INFERNAL TRAMPS

It began along a derelict stretch of railroad tracks. Far from known depots and their nightwatchmen's midnight roustings. I lived in the wooded foothills overlooking the rails, sleeping out of doors, as is the wont of men with troubled hearts and an illimitable fondness for corn whiskey.

A cupolaed caboose rolled to a stop on the tracks below, appearing as if from nothing. It drifted through the air in a tangled mist. It did not breach shadow or break the fog but materialized into substance and form. A lighthouse gallery rose out of the coalescing railroad car's roof.

Two dim crimson dots dilated into firelit rubies blurrily flickering behind the cupola window.

There were other windows below the cupola's, along the outer walls of the caboose, full of inert gloom.

I heard pneumatics hiss as release valves were let. The rear door of the caboose slid open, and even from my far remove I could smell the meaty reek of carcasses' rot. An oil lantern mounted beside the sliding door shone over a long-limbed hunchback emerging from the car wearing a belted wrap coat, bringing with her a bouquet of oil heat, hookbait, and outhouse shit.

Her hands were three times the length and girth of human hands. The top of her head almost kissed the railcar's roof. Her chest moved up and down, the movement more mechanical than biological, under her wrap's ragged drape.

She untied the belt of her coat, letting the front panels fall sidelong away from the gnarled humps of her naked body. Slung from her chest were translucent mammaries interiorly mapped out in visible branches of black veins. Each breast undulated with a liquid volume of its own separate tempo.

The gruesome mistress picked up a bundle concealed nearby. The cry of an infant child escaped its cotton sling.

She let the bundle fall to the ground from where she stood on the end platform. I choked on my tongue.

But I did nothing. All who hide are wont to never do. And a drunk who lives alone out of doors is hiding. Even if, permitting a tired cliché, I was only hiding from myself.

———

THE SMALLEST DREADS SOAK MY BONES. BE IT THE PARANOID certainty of being watched in a grocery store line, the nagging thought of an unknown debt, a vague notion of some undiagnosable illness coring out my organs. My fears are in my marrow.

I am a filthy wretch, roaming. That is the sort of man I've come to be.

I did not go to the infant once dropped by its nursemaid. I did not even go down the same night the child was dropped. I waited until there was no doubt the nightmarish harpy had cut and run. Waited wary as a rat.

It was halfway through morning that I had liquid courage enough to slide down the hillside. I searched the ballast and surrounding muck-swollen swale near where I'd seen the child dropped.

The bundle lay open but empty. No, that couldn't be. I know I'd heard it. Though, what exactly had I heard?

Because I'd been leaning too long on my bootleg crutch to rule out auditory hallucinations. Too many moons of moonshine, bringing florid psychosis to bloom. There were other terrible possibilities, of course. The kid could've been snatched up by the local wildlife. If it'd been dropped from the railcar, it surely would've wailed long and hard enough for something hungry to hear its wailing.

Neither fox nor bobcat shouldn't delight in so easy a meal.

At any rate, I went to go look.

———

I FOUND IT STRANDED JUST PAST THE RIPRAP RANGED AROUND the tracks. It crawled, body slick with slime, out of a discarded oil drum. What it was I couldn't say, but not a normal human infant. It overtook the drum's lip and snail-trailed down the barrel. Left a streak of placental mucus the color of marmalade.

Its outsized head was (more or less) anatomically complete. There were ears and there were eyes and there were teeth, lips, and nose. But its head had the smooth indistinction of a mannequin's head. Its body was scaled smaller than its skull, limbs with more tendons outside than in, braided into a collagen exoskeleton. Its whole anatomy was overlaid with a translucent, chrysalid husk. What I took for its genitals were livid purple.

It managed to stand, though the weight of its head sent it teetering. It immediately fell back down to the ground. This happened several times before it managed to keep upright.

I stripped my ragged overcoat and bundled the creature back up as it stood. Its body seemed unable to bear even the bare weight of wool. The overcoat dragged the creature to the ground like it was sinking into quicksand; bewildered. It projected both the humiliation of a dog who's had an accident on the rug and the pickled stupefaction of a disorderly drunk teenager arrested while traveling abroad.

It was terribly pathetic.

I was a coward, but not without compassion. I picked up the creature and carried it uphill to my campsite.

I'll admit, I'd grown lonely in my long reclusion, and thought myself just as terribly pathetic, if in my own way, as this helpless little freak.

A malformed runt and a boozehound. Quite the pack of strays.

————

I DECIDED THE GHOUL AND HER PHANTOM RAILCAR WERE anathemas of my delusion. More of gravy than of grave. So I got about the business of my weird ward's upbringing.

I nurtured the runt with soft food such as was available to a drifter of no worldly means, cooking camp-fired canned beans, grinding trail mix with evaporated milk to improvise unhazardous pap.

To its nourishment I added amusement, plying the orphan with tales of my youth: of adolescence's backseat fumblings, heavy petting and handprints behind fogged windows at movie theatre drive-ins, hot and heavy summers under the enchantment of state fairs' cabochon bulbs and calliope sounds, totems of light and noise against sour-faced puritans perennially bedeviled by "the haunting fear that someone, somewhere, may be happy." We showed a promise only youth, ignorant of that promise while abusing its privileges, can demonstrate by virtue of their mindless gumption. I peppered in my adulthood's minor triumphs, scant though they'd been, touching on my brief tenure teaching, omitting the later backsliding that brought the abyss right to my heels.

The creature attended to my tales, a child enraptured. It could not comprehensibly speak, but would repeat what I said, refining fluidity and rhythm as a percussionist rehearsing rudiments. It aped me as it could, felt the shape of my words on its own tongue. It grasped at every trifling sound.

If I laughed, it laughed. If I sighed, it sighed.

It did a passable imitation of my brooding silence.

Its pantomimes became overeager and then sometimes disquieting. A dog with a human voice box, but no corresponding complex thought.

Its deformity aroused my charity where I should have expected disgust, as if I'd awakened to what once drove saints to dress lepers' wounds.

The creature was not of me, but I treated it as my own, reserving to it the best of my beggarly things. Each night I tucked it in its brand-new sleeping bag I'd stolen from the military surplus while on a bender out and about town. I painstakingly built it our tented haven, beginning by firming up a foundation of groundsheet and pads. I swathed the walls in diamond-stitched moving blankets, tightened the guy lines, replanted stakes through the grommets to tauten the tent into homier shape.

I offered it a respectable sense of place despite our straitened circumstance. I fed the runt better than I'd ever eaten, whether in lean times or plenty. Gave it what I remembered of my mother's own tenderness. Found a nobler purpose than fueling the death drive that motored my ceaseless dissipation along. I was not born a nihilist, I started to remember.

And somehow my best efforts, shabby though they'd been, met with appreciable results.

Over several weeks, its body fattened and ruddied, became distinguishably male. He was as a gaunt stoutening on the mend. Cadaverous cheekbones filled out, no longer an internment camp escapee's. His skull's size and sharp cast diminished in proportion to his growing appetite.

Then came an unlikely wonder. "My name is Varick," he one day said without explanation, without prompting on my part.

I was stunned. But well-pleased, of course. "I'm Jerome," I said, without questioning the miracle. I was aware of the poor form of looking a gift horse in its mouth.

———

WE SAT A WELL-SPOKEN WEEK TOGETHER AROUND THE FIRE, enlivened by Varick's newfound fluency and his discovery of booze. He'd found my same relish for rotgut. I was as Abbé Faria embracing Edmond Dantès in *The Count of Monte Cristo*: "You are my son, Dantès. You are the child of my captivity."

Orphans, however, can only be nurtured to a behavioral threshold. Nature is apt to steamroll habit. Blood being thicker than water, and all.

I began noticing some of Varick's peculiarities.

He became violently ill after eating. But never threw up his food. He instead heaved from his gut the same marmaladian gunge through which he'd slimed out the drum.

Varick starkened, grew unnaturally aged. His demeanor harshened. His jaw was strong, nose hard and almost hooked, hair and boar-bristle-thick mustache the begrimed silver of battered old jail cell bars. His body, a hunched raptor's, vulturine and wiry. I imagined his hands as carrion-caked claws. He radiated hunger for food other than that I could bring.

He didn't doze but shammed sleep, cocooning in his sleeping bag at the same hour I turned in; I couldn't help but be unnerved by it. Breaking the surface of my night terrors, sleeping bag drenched with sweat, I'd find Varick eyeing me from his corner. In my nightmares I woke into other nightmares. This set me at irreality's dubious vantage.

Dreamt of waking at the witching hour, Varick feeding on stinking offal by my berth, chin bedewed by the maggoty mincemeat of roadkill. Dreamt him whispering conspiracy to fat-gutted vultures dressed in fleshy caruncles and wattles. They spoke German and in raucous laughter, catcalling deformed biergarten-girls in threadbare dirndls wildly dancing through my dreams; their talons pinched glass tankards the size of children's beach buckets, filled with human blood instead of lager. Their sharp beaks sneered impossible grins.

On my waking—though I could not remember waking —Varick spoke not only more fluently than he had yet to do, but now also spoke German. He possessed an inexplicable mastery of Teutonic idiom. (*"Da steppt der Bär"*—"the bear is dancing there"—amongst other pith.)

This sudden polyglossia disturbed me more deeply than had his phantasmagoric arrival into my world.

Thereafter the divide between dreaming and wakefulness surrendered itself to a broader hypnogogic state. Any real thing, simulacra; unreality, materially real. I couldn't be sure I hadn't seen what I thought I had, or exactly when it was that I had seen it, whatever it was that I had (or had not) seen.

If that's confusing, so much more so for me.

I felt the air shiver. The wind was full of omens.

———

"I'M HEADED TO TOWN TO BUY HOOCH," I SAID TO VARICK. "Tagging along?"

"*Nein, nein.* I will stay here. Soon they are coming."

"Who?"

Varick smiled and said, "You shall see."

———

I FOLLOWED THE RAILWAY'S RETURN ROUTE FROM TOWN, hoofed it back uphill.

I heard throaty laughter once I'd trudged halfway up the foothills. Pushed through the wall of scrubland and spruce concealing our camp. Tangerine pixels pierced the thicket, pinpoints of firelight scattering the bush, will-o'-the-wisps prancing through the shrub. I tasted illusion binding its noise and light in gusts of smoke. Was swallowed in the stew of strangers' laughter. Violence simmered in their kettle, waiting to boil over to brutality from glee. My feet wouldn't carry me back the way that I came.

Time skipped—I melted through the bush. My legs moved by the operation of an extrinsic force. There they were, sat around the blazing kindling and cordwood, each eyeing the flames' flickering, strange sway.

"Jerome, *mein Freund*…town…*war es gut?*"

A band of dead ringers, all arranged around the bonfire. Above the neck, the three others were Varick's doppelgängers. Each, the same brute face, hair and mustache bristling cold hoosegow-gray. The lookalikes were meatier than Varick, beef and brawn below the chin, square shoulders and big, barreled chests. I supposed this was my runt's imagined lost litter.

"I got Dickel white corn whiskey," I said to justify myself. I held up the bottle wrapped in brown paper inside a plastic bag.

"*Gut, gut,*" Varick said. "We are just waiting on the others."

One doppelgänger eased himself my way to commandeer the bottle. My resistance was brief. He wrapped his fingers around my own as I held the corn whiskey's bottleneck. He patted my hand as a sweet-natured grandfather counseling unruly offspring. "*Alles gut. Ich werde mich darum kümmern.*"

"Yes, yes," Varick said, repeating, "we are just waiting on the others."

"Oh. Who else is coming? I…" trailed off despite a nervous compulsion to talk.

"*Sie kehren zurück.* They come now," another doppelgänger said. The brutes moved their heads and looked in perfect tandem toward the footfalls of nearby approach.

So came a small congress of fellow tramps and rummies, escorted by three more changelings astride the flanks. Tramps shuffled in around the fire. Like labrats rolled into sleepboxes after their last circuit through the maze.

They all stared at either their feet or far away.

"*Sieben Brüder, vereint zum Fest!*" Varick said. His six strapping brethren howled.

"I been to Germany once," the eldest bum broke in. He had yellow in his gray beard. The yellow could've been thatches of ginger bleached blonde by the sun. The yellow could've been an unwashed residue of nicotine and grunge. He had yellow in his teeth, under his fingernails, on his tongue. The only unyellow thing about him was the bedraggled drab olive of his field jacket and trousers. "Used to be in the service," he said, as if explaining his fatigues.

Several winos babbled assent such as each was inclined to offer. "I lived in Yorkville when I was a kid. Lots'a German bakeries," said one. "I met a black feller h'was born in Berlin," said another.

"I used to live in *Deutschland* m'self," the eldest bum said. "Stationed in Kaiserslautern."

"And what of our mother tongue, soldier?" Varick's eyes slyly sought out his brothers, sniggering into their chests.

"Never learnt. They learnt English."

The sternest changeling chided his half-dozen kin. "*Genug. Es ist Zeit, die Landstreicher zu essen.*" A despotic father's cadence, brooking no dissent.

"Goddamnit!" A rummy, kept silent till now, spat at his own feet, lips curling in a sneer peculiar to a lifetime of disaffection compounded by drink. Corners of the rummy's eyes bore thorned wrinkles creeping over the angrily swollen bags beneath them, as if decades of unceasing agitation seeped through his flesh. Tear ducts gummy, watery gut almost gestationally round, eyes jaundice-yellow but for the burst capillaries puddling his sclera cheap-lipstick-red. "Is we here to get hammered, or is we ain't? All this unholy horseshit. I says it's time we get loose, Fritz. Fuckin' fish or cut bait."

Varick and brethren hauled weighted glances between them. One who'd relieved me of the whiskey bottle brought it to Varick, put it in his hand. The gold-and-white shrink band, a telltale for tampering, was stripped off the finish. I saw the marmaladian gunge dissolve inside. It didn't prompt me to act, and I can't say why it should not have done.

Varick held the bottle to the agitator. "Here, *Bruder*," he said, "the first sacrament is yours. *Fürchtet uns, die Gefallenen, anstelle eures Gottes.*"

"Sounds like a prayer," the eldest bum said. "That a prayer?"

The agitator swiped the bottle from Varick's hand and hollered "Hallelujah!" Then tore himself off a tenacious guzzle.

Everyone else would drink in their turn.

———

THAT NIGHT I DREAMT OF SEVEN VULTURES. THEY ROOSTED around a circle of dying trees, the branches overhanging a midden teeming with rats.

———

A SMOLDERING FIRE, DEAD CENTER OF THE UNPEOPLED campsite. Sky swarming with nautical twilight's liminal gloom, night swirling away against the skyward crawl of day.

I heard eruptions of hooligan laughter. They trailed away in a Doppler shift blunted by the morning mist.

My head ached. Shreds of gamy meat soaked in alcohol and sleep wedged in my teeth and gums. An outfit I'd once gave Varick was now neatly folded beside the smoldering fire, beside six other tidy stacks of clothes.

One of them cried out in the distance: "*Zögern Sie nicht! Mutter wird bald kommen!*"

I chased their hollering down the holler and cut out toward the rails.

I saw the caboose and stopped at its sight. The hideous mistress, there, waiting, already unwrapped, beastly in the buff on the platformed backend. Her translucent breasts, bloated monstrosities, gallons of blood sloshing around coal-black plexuses inside.

Peals of guttural laughter escaped the railcar, whose side windows' quondam dim dormancy was now peopled with sharp profiles wading through yellow light. Waves of sound beat against me. The world, filled up with a bawdy, Hunnic din. Might've been dozens of them crying out. Some shrilled, some roared, some at a higher or lower pitch. All a common timbre, each colored a different shade of Varick's same voice.

I spotted (my) Varick by the embryonic fragility persisting in his delicate limbs. Him and his siblings hobbled buck naked, bellies glut unto distension, coming close to the caboose. All in the altogether, each carrying a wet burlap sack, jute bottoms leaking red Rorschach trails in the dirt.

Varick waited to be last up the platform. The other brothers trod the staircase in sequence as they surrendered their bloody haul. Their infernal mother took and held all half-dozen carcassed sacks' combined weight, took them in a single hand, expending not an ounce of effort. Each brother gave her a peck on the unsightly cheek and, relinquishing his tribute, entered the caboose. Their brethren's frenzied celebration received the returnees from within.

The other half-dozen having already joined the doghouse revelry, Varick mounted the platform steps. He stopped halfway, like a commuter who'd dropped his billfold hearing a sudden Good Samaritan yell after him. I watched, not knowing…

Varick turned and faced me. Naked body, glistening with gristle; silver-gray mustache stained deep, gory red. While one stick-thin arm gripped the top of the oversized sack slung over his shoulder and pressed against his back, he raised his free hand, and with a smile on his face, he waved.

Through my tears I smiled back at him. I waved back. I waved goodbye.

They really do grow up so fast.

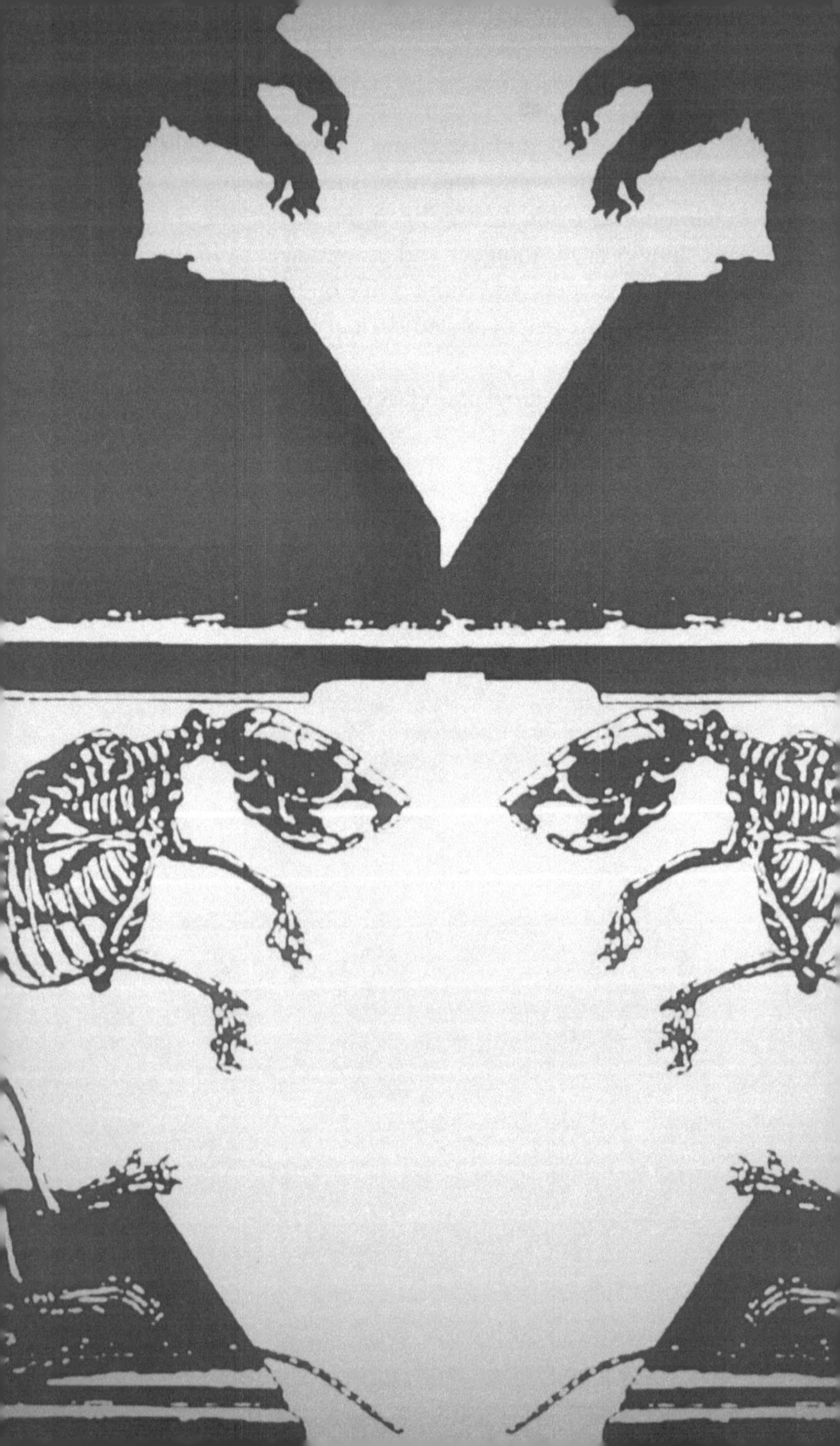

RATS

An Influx of Vermin

There's a nasty dead rat on the tabletop. It's dried out, like roadkill left on a desert road during a drought. A balloon-shaped snifter hits the table, the burning spoon goes flying, and cognac soaks the rat's tail. The air is dense with fumes like old furniture and dried fruit. The rat's tail fattens like a dry paper towel eating up a spill.

No one else watches, no one else notices, but fascination keeps his eyes on the rat. There's a creaking sound like a branch groaning just before it breaks. The rat's eyes open to look straight at him.

A Wriggling Purge

The woman's flesh looked like someone unevenly scraped off her eyebrows, scalped her, dragged her lips from her face. I've seen her walking outside Emory University. Today I saw her when I pulled into the Headquarters' parking lot off of Clifton Road. I stopped my car and rolled down the window. There aren't that many people to talk to anymore; beggars can't be choosers.

"Afternoon," I said.

The woman smiled. Then started retching. I was paralyzed by the sight of her mouth spewing out rats.

The Bubonic Transfiguration

People used to kill each other over this place. There's blood in the stones, soaked into the ground. The sun rises over the temple wall. It reminds the boy of the floating ball illusion; the sun, a magician's ball, the limestone wall a two-thousand year old rag.

The boy thought he was the only one alive who didn't have a furred worm of a tail. Then, the old man came and started praying. With each day of supplication, his head worn raw from pressing it to the stones, the old man changed. He became like everything else: vermin.

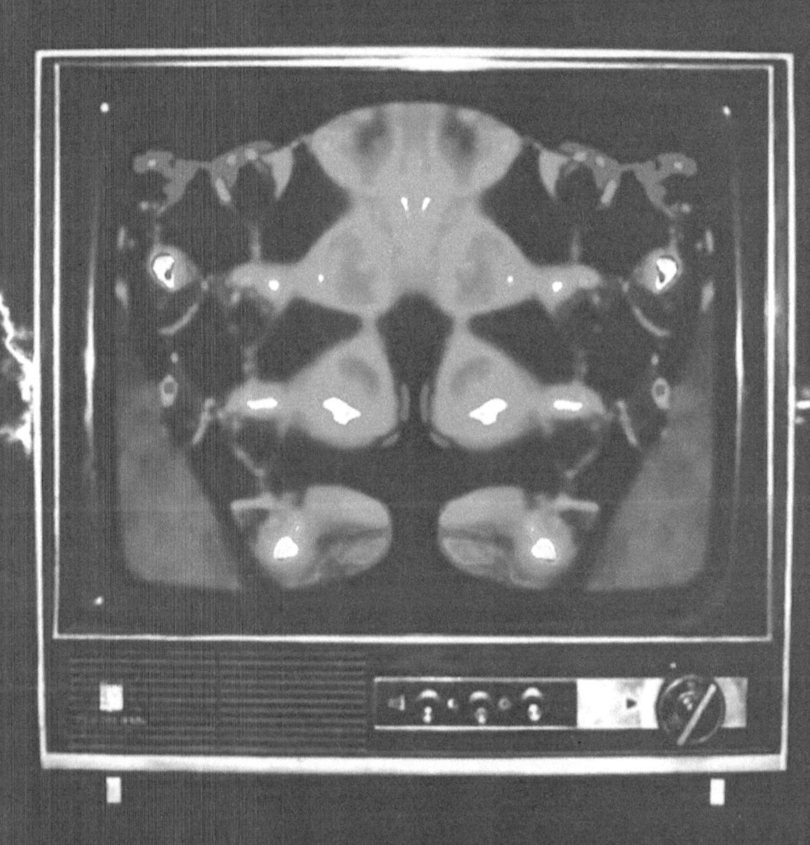

PUJKAMAUNKA SPLASH

D o you remember the game Pujkamaunka Splash?
I do.

Not that there weren't memorable events aplenty in 1993. Clinton was inaugurated. Jurassic Park was in theaters. The ATF botching the Waco Siege.

And me? A kid has kid dreams, of course.

I'd been saving up for a new Mongoose Villain freestyle bike. After a friend showed me a homemade video of Mat Hoffman doing tailwhips and tabletops, I'd become a BMX ramp-riding nut. I was destined for California and super-stardom, a life of rad stunts and sun-kissed bleach-blonde beach-bunnies loving all over me until I was almost sick of it (almost).

But all that was pushed aside when they announced the release date for Pujkamaunka Splash. I never did buy that bike.

I have memories of me and all the other middle-schoolers saying "we're going Puji", of tearing ads out of GamePro magazine and geeking out over them, not under-standing that marketing wasn't the product itself. A game's graphics could only blow your mind as far as sixteen bits would let it, and back then that wasn't very far.

But you say that you don't remember it. I guess I'm not surprised. Nobody ever does. Nobody can find it, can even find any mention of the game. And if you Google it—and go ahead, right now, if you've got the time, so you can see I'm not lying—you won't find it. You'll find a YouTube video about Splash World Punta Cana and a TikTok about puka lava backsplashes.

But nothing about the game.

Why does nobody but me remember Pujkamaunka Splash?

———

THE PLAN WAS FOR MY GRANDFATHER TO BRING ME AND MY dog Pistol in his Country Squire station wagon to the Bavaria Galleria mall.

He picked us up out front of my mom's tract house, our wild yard littered with my baby sister's Fisher-Price toys and a Slip 'N Slide that never got put away. Our neighbors hated us.

It was early in the morning when Grandpa showed up, early enough that the streetlamps were still on. Mom watched me get into his car from the TV room window.

Me and Pistol sat in the back. I felt funny sitting up front with my grandfather so I always tried to avoid it. When I irritated him, he said things like, "Stop being trouble or I'll leave you where trouble lives. With the poor kids."

To which I would reply, "Mom says we are the poor kids."

"I mean the ones with fleas. You ever eat nothing but cold cheese and knuckle sandwiches?"

I didn't know if he was serious. I made sure I didn't push him far enough to find out.

———

We got to the Bavaria Galleria at about seven in the morning. The sun was only just coming out and the line was already hundreds of people long, stretching from the mall entrance all the way up the sidewalk that snaked around the lot.

This was a bad sign. Grandpa hated three things more than anything else in this world—Japanese cars, fake cripples parking in real cripples' handicapped spaces, and waiting in lines.

He looked back at me through the rearview mirror while I tried to wipe the frown off my face. I didn't want this whole ride to be for nothing. I figured he'd seen the line and we were just going to drive back home.

But he looked at me in the rearview and grinned a co-conspirator's grin. "Don't worry, kid. We're not waiting in line."

We pulled up to a reinforced door next to a loading dock and dumpsters, and got out of the car.

"Hey Sam," an elderly security guard said to my grandpa, "how's tricks?"

"Hanging further port than starboard, but at least the wedding tackle's still operational. Not that anything's biting. This is my grandson, Trevor. Trevor, this is my buddy Spetz."

"Nice to meet you, Mr. Spetz," I said, and shuffled Pistol's leash over to my left hand so I could offer a handshake.

"Just Spetz, kid," he said, shaking my hand. "That's quite a grip you got." He leaned in toward Grandpa and nudged him in the ribs. "Kid's been practicing the five-knuckle shuffle, huh?"

"Easy, Spetz."

"I'm just joshing you."

"I know, Spetz. If you were serious, you'd be collecting your teeth."

———

Spetz deposited me, grandpa, and my dog Pistol right out front of Babbage's. There was a younger guard holding our place in line; he left right when we showed up. I looked around at the other adult chaperones fencing in the queue of teens and pre-teens waiting to get in. Everyone had shown up with their grandparents. All of them were younger than sixteen or older than sixty.

Behind us, there were fluorescent lights the same color as a dirty pool looks underwater. Near those were little tiled plant beds interspersed with random shrubbery, benches for husbands to park themselves, bistro tables favored by shrieky gossipers.

In front of us was a huddle of men in coveralls and workcoats, trucker caps and beanies, all of them laced up in workboots. I couldn't tell just what they were doing. They all stood around a big wishing well, yelling at the fountain in the middle of it.

"What are they doing over there?" I asked.

"Where?" Grandpa said.

"Right there." I pointed.

Grandpa looked up from his newspaper. "It's just an empty fountain." He brought the paper back up in front of his face. "They're probably waiting on someone to fix it."

"You don't see those guys?" I said.

Grandpa peeked over his paper again and stared right where I was pointing. He looked long enough that he couldn't have missed it. But he still showed no sign that he'd seen what I saw. He reached in his slacks. I heard his pockets jangle. He pulled out a few dimes, a quarter, a dozen pennies. He gave me one of the pennies. "Go ahead, make a wish."

I started in the direction of the wishing well, but Grandpa put his hand on my shoulder. "Leave the dog," he said.

"You don't mind watching him?"

"Leave the dog." He sounded the way people who go a long time without sleep sound. I handed him the leash.

I walked over to the wishing well, nudging between two bearded tanks with beerbellies and acid reflux breath. The fountain had been emptied out. I could see two pitbull mixes in the dry well, baring their teeth and snapping and growling at each other.

Someone shoved into someone else who then shoved into me, bumping me into one of the beerbellied human tanks. Malt liquor spilled in my hair and down my back, reeking somewhere between candy-flavored medicine and fresh-cut sheet-metal. All the men held either a tallboy or a bottle. The well reeked of cheap swill and sweat-soaked workclothes.

A drunk maintenance man was yelling himself hoarse. "I want to see a throat out, show me a mutt'll rip another's throat out!" The others cheered. A cloud of cigarette smoke grew or dissipated in proportion to the drunken noise. It seemed like all the men together were one organism breathing smoke and alcoholic fumes. Some slapped each other's backs with cigarettes or beer still held in their hands. Sparks flew from embers as rough fingers struck burning cherries; cans of Schlitz malt liquor and Old Style bashed lips and sloshed beer on uniforms; bottles were smashed on the ground when one of the dogs edged in on the other.

One of the pitbulls got the other by the throat, The men

cheered, spewing raucous noise the color of blue-gray smoke from their mouths. One pitbull necked the other and I covered my face. The weaker dog whined and squealed; it sounded like when Mom dropped a paint can on Pistol's foot, but worse. I felt rough hands on me, hands that smelled like grease and piss and drugstore liquor; the hands grabbed my face and vise-gripped my skull and forced me to look forward. A phlegmy voice croaked in my ear, "Watch it, boy. Watch, now. This is where he takes the cunting throat."

I was terrified.

I thrashed at the stranger's hands. I struggled free. I shoved at every meaty, sweat-stinking body around me. No one tried to stop me. I wasn't even remotely as interesting as dogs killing dogs.

I came back and stood in line. My grandfather wasn't reading the paper. Now he was just fidgeting, checking his wristwatch. It took him a half-minute to notice me. When he looked down, I handed him back the penny and said, "I didn't use it."

I thought for sure Grandpa would notice that I was shaken up, but he didn't say anything, only took the penny and gave me back Pistol's leash.

Cheering started up the line, a rippling daisy chain of applause. I looked ahead: they were opening the store.

———

WHEN IT WAS YOUR TURN, A MAN WITH A MOUTHLESS AND eye-holeless bag over his head unhooked a red velvet rope to let you in. One kid at a time.

The black bag over the man's head was sackcloth. The velvet rope, shabby and stain-spotted. Baghead's body was scoliotic and knobby, flesh-pinks hued gray by time, prune-wrinkly like hourlong-bathtub-fingers. He was so, so old—much older than my grandpa, than any of the others waiting on line with their grandkids—I could tell even with his face covered.

I was next. The ancient baghead came close to shouting at me. "Give your dog to your minder and hold out your hand." His voice was a soundboard of reptile noises and pneumonic respiration, punctuated by a hack and growl here, a cough and grumble there. He spoke an alien English; the syllables and consonants were in their proper place and his diction was spot-on, but it was phonetically mysticized, shifting words I ought to have known into something foreign and new.

"Give up the goddamned leash, I said, you scuttling little whelp." Baghead's wretched voice was more powerful than a man's half his age.

I looked up at my grandpa, expecting him to give a lipful right back. But, as I held the leash out (with my very nervy and whining poodle attached to it) for him to take, Grandpa stared at the sickly glowing fluorescents overhead, a small spot of drool pooling the corner of his mouth.

"You go wait there," the baghead said to—no, commanded—my grandfather, bouncing his bagged head at a gaggle of grandparents huddled by a shelf filled with Super Mario All-Stars and other Nintendo properties. They were all gray and bent, even grayer and further bent because they were here.

Grandpa pulled Pistol over to the seniors' huddle. He bent down on one knee to gently pet our family dog. He'd never pet Pistol before. I couldn't move. I had a sense of the uncanny, something strange and powerful changing the air we breathed, the blood in our veins, strange and powerful enough to make men do things they wouldn't otherwise do.

I was gobsmacked to see a very young girl (the only one who wasn't there to buy the game) bring Pistol a stainless steel dish to drink from. Her head was roughly shaved, the whole skull scabbed in congealed red chicken scratch. And she was completely nude.

———

I DON'T KNOW HOW WE KNEW NOT TO TELL OUR PARENTS (OR anyone) what we did in that room behind the black curtain. I don't know that my memories of the day I bought Pujkamaunka Splash, or the day after, or all the days after that, would make sense to anyone but me. Because they weren't memories. Not really. They were sensations and images, echoes of acts:

A bright green screen on the largest cathode-ray TV I'd ever seen, blood oozing from between the screen's glass and the TV housing; sun-flare-bright lights flash-frying my retinas; a cold, bone hand wrapped around my wrist, a steel hammer held inside my fingers.

Urinating on the floor, howling along with my dog Pistol, while a carpet-wide bed of worms, their wriggling bodies so dark-green they were almost black, noisily slushed and squirted as they crawled over the body of another naked girl. I think she'd died before the worms wetly groped her.

I saw the giant TV's screen split and crackle open, glass shards for teeth and dark-green ooze like drool, the broken mouth wailing in animal anguish so terrible that Pistol lost his legs, a puddle of urine spreading underneath him on the floor.

After that, nothing. I remembered nothing until we'd got to the car.

———

WE SAT IN THE STATION WAGON, MY COPY OF PUJKAMAUNKA Splash resting on the dashboard in front of me. It was like I'd only just woken up.

My hands were stained red and there were bloodied strings of curly white fur in between my fingers. I looked over at Grandpa still holding Pistol's leash. Pistol was gone. Grandpa softly cried through a bloody nose and split lip he hadn't had before.

My grandfather was in the 20th Armored Division when the US Army liberated the Dachau concentration camp. I'd never seen him cry before.

I went home and I played my game. I never saw my grandfather again.

———

SO NOW YOU UNDERSTAND THE MYSTIQUE, THE VIOLENCE— the sheer, ruining lust of Pujkamaunka. Though you can't trust what I say. How could you? A video game that dominated the market for years and then disappeared without anyone anywhere remembering any of it? I might as well say I'm the King of England.

And even though I was the only one who remembered the game, I didn't understand my memories of it. Not until I found the game again, hidden after all these years.

I blew the dust from the cartridge. I wiped down the Super Nintendo. I put the game cartridge in. And I started to play.

And my television opened its mouth, like the TV in Babbage's did more than thirty years ago. And inside my television's mouth, I could hear them calling out for me. From deep inside Pujkamaunka Splash, I heard them. I heard Pistol, and I heard Grandpa. And I heard the ancient baghead, too. They were telling me something.

I heard that strange voice, that bagheaded voice speaking a once-incomprehensible language, an alien tongue I now understood:

"The time is right. Now bring others to play."

A WOMAN OF DISTINCTION

D o I kill often? No, not often.
(Stop touching that window, it doesn't open, and it doesn't even go anywhere.)

I don't need to kill often, and I don't do things I don't need to do, unless I'm paid to. Once every two months is enough; killing once every two months works just fine for me.

(You can stop crying, the walls are soundproofed.)

Six slayings-per-annum is sufficient to regenerate my dying cells, purge the cancerous ones, slough off aging flesh —and then I'm young again. Well, physically.

(Quit trying that door, it's not like there's anything out there. It's called "the woods" for a reason.)

To be young-at-heart is as much perspective as it is smooth skin and gravity-resistant breasts.

(It's very nice that you want to apologize now, but you'll forgive me, given the circumstances, if I don't credit your apology as genuine. And no, I won't be letting you go. If you get the same answer over and over, why keep asking the same question?)

To be young-at-heart would require that I regather the suppositions of my youth. But at five-hundred years old, it's a bit too late for that. The world I was born into was a very different place. I grew up in the Rhineland at the dawn of the sixteenth century; *Malleus Maleficerum* was at the top of the bestseller list and people thought Jews controlled the weather. (Okay, so in some ways, not much has changed.) Dowries still included livestock. Marriage still included dowries!

(I set out tea and cookies on that table bolted to the floor. But if you have any other reasonable last requests, I'll consider them. Remember that the operative word is "reasonable".)

And I can't roll back time any more than I can turn into a hamster.

(Yes, I know, it's very good tea. No, I don't want to see a picture of your mother.)

You must believe me—and I mean this, really, I do—that I don't enjoy killing.

But if I'm supposed to finish the book I've been writing for the last two-hundred years, I must tend to my nutrition. One can't draw blood from a stone.

(Why feed you? Well, I'm just being a good hostess. Just because I'm going to kill you doesn't mean I forget my manners.)

What's the book about? Well, it's what you might call "conduct literature". Think of a modern version of Tannhäuser's *Book of Manners*, or *Book of the Civilized Man* by Daniel of Beccles.

You see, I've spent a half-millennium dealing with snotty little shits just like you. Chucklefucks who like to spill beer on my cocktail dress and laugh about it with their friends like a coffle of imbecilic donkeys. And it's high time for reeducating the vulgarians, the hooligans, the philistines. Think how much longer your life would be if you'd been forewarned that gentlemanliness can safeguard your physical safety.

The name of the book? I think I'm going to call it *How Being Rude Can Get You Killed*. I'd let you read it, but you won't be around.

(Yes, you're going in the book.)

ODD EGG

There was a man waiting for me on my front porch when I got home from work. He waved at me as I walked up my driveway to my house. I had a strange feeling about him, because he was a strange-looking man. There are strangers, and then there are strange strangers, and there's a world of difference between them. But I waved back.

"Good evening," I said.

"And to you," the man said. His head was shaped like an egg. It was almost one-third taller than the average man's head.

"Can I help you?" I said.

"Let me not be rude," he said. "It's my pleasure to make your acquaintance. In the way of comity and fellowship, I'd like to introduce myself. My name is Roger." He held out for a handshake.

I shook his hand. His fingers were long and cold and bumpy. A strange stranger's strange head and strange hands.

"Roger, I'm Maryellen," I said. "Let me also not be rude but still be direct. I've had a long day at work. Maybe you could come right out and tell me what you're doing here and how I can help you."

Eggheaded Roger nodded like I'd said something true and wise. "I can certainly appreciate that. If there's something that I can appreciate, it's directness. That's what folks are missing these days, directness. That, along with a direction. I'm a rather direct man myself," he said, though in the middle of disproving the same, "so let me get right to it." He bent down and reached into a paper grocery bag. Then pulled out a carton of eggs. "I'm from the Keystone Co-operative Growers Association, and I would like to offer you these eggs. They're farm-fresh and cruelty-free. And it would be my honor, and the honor of my fellow growers, if you would accept this gift and use these eggs to your own delight."

He held out the carton. I took the eggs. "Oh. Oh, okay. This is like a—this is a—what is this?"

"A carton of eggs, ma'am." His smile was too wide for his face, and it looked like the gesture was hurting him.

"Yes, I understand that part—"

"Good," he said.

"—but why are you giving out free eggs?"

"This is just a service we provide to the community. You see, the KCGA—that's our initialism, for brevity's sake, you understand—the KCGA's position is that to enjoy a good egg is to enjoy life. We want the whole world to enjoy their lives, which to some degree means we want them to enjoy our eggs, too!"

"Oh."

"Do you know that a god lives inside of our eggs?"

"How's that now?"

"The time will come when the god-filled eggs will feed the sick and the poor until the sick and the poor are no more. That time will be the Time of the Egg. Everything unborn will be born and everything dead will be born again. All will fall under the judgment of the Many Heads."

I stared at him. I said, "Is this a religious thing? I'm not really much of a churchgoer…"

"There will be no more faith when the world's flags are blooded by the Many Heads. The light of sanctification is kept only inside the egg."

"I've only ever met one Scientologist. Are you a Scien—"

"Well, as I said, it would make all of us at the KCGA just happy as the day is long if you'd only take those eggs and enjoy them for yourself. And with that, I will leave you and wish you a wonderful rest of your evening. Enjoy your eggs, and enjoy your life, ma'am. And if you can, enjoy both at once!"

He turned and sprinted toward the woods. I looked down at my carton of eggs, thinking of L. Ron Hubbard.

———

THE KCGA MAN WAS HALF A BUBBLE OFF PLUMB, AND I WAS undecided as far as eating lunatic produce. I thought I'd mull it over before frying up the man's eggs.

But maybe I was being mistrustful. I reminded myself to keep in the habit of having faith in people until they gave me a reason not to.

———

I WOKE UP HUNGRY SATURDAY MORNING. STILL IN MY pajamas, I maundered downstairs with the residue of sleep in my eyes. I looked in my refrigerator. There was nothing in there but KCGA eggs.

I picked the egg carton up out of the refrigerator. I put the eggs on the counter next to where the range was built in. I took the salted butter from the fridge and lobbed off a dollop into the skillet. I clicked the gas on the stovetop. The skillet got crackling. I reached for one of the eggs.

I picked up the first egg, nice and cold from the fridge. I could feel the weight of albumen and yolk inside the shell. But when I broke open the shell on the edge of the skillet, nothing came out.

I felt like one of those rubes a magician calls on stage just to make fun of. Nobody likes a tricksy egg for breakfast.

I picked up the next one, holding the heft of a shell full of egg. I again split it on the skillet. Naught but nothing, the same as before.

There I was, starting to get miffed.

I went through eleven eggs that way. I felt a chicken embryo sloshing around inside every shell—hell, I know what a full egg feels like. I cracked almost all of them open; empty down to a one.

One egg was left. In for a penny, in for a pound: I picked up what I expected to be the last empty egg. Except when I cracked this one, something came out.

It wasn't the yolk.

An egg-shaped human head plopped skittering into the skillet. It had two sets of three little legs, a set coming out each side of the head. I screeched, and when the spidery little head hit the skillet and started sizzling, it started screeching, too.

I took the spatula and flipped the thing onto the counter. It moved its spindly little legs in purposeless panic. Cried, like how a baby cries. A tiny little egg-sized critter, half-fried on my kitchen counter.

I turned off the burner. I had no idea what to do next.

The six-legged-head made a wheezing sound, followed by a noise like air being let out of a bicycle tire. And then it was dead.

I did not shower or brush my teeth or put real clothes on or do any of the things I'd earlier planned to do. I poured myself three fingers of whisky, grabbed the pack of cigarettes I'd swore off two months ago, and parked my ass on my front porch stoop. I sat there until I'd finished my whisky and smoked a half-dozen Parliaments.

I tucked my old-fashioned glass behind my derrière when the early risers passed by on their morning stroll. To neighbors who stopped and said they thought I'd quit smoking, I made a gesture of hey-what-can-you-do.

———

I HAD SOME LIQUID COURAGE TO FORTIFY ME, SO I reentered my house and went back in my kitchen.

The six-legged-head was gone. But there was another egg in its place. This one was about the size of a grapefruit.

———

I FIGURED ON DRIVING DOWN THE STATE ROAD TO MY FRIEND Dustin's. His daddy was a poultryman, so Dustin knew lots about chickens and lots about eggs and loved talking about both. So much so that I'd previously found him duller than watching paint dry. But it's not like I ever told him.

I put the big egg in a little grocery bag and hung it on the wall hooks while I got ready to see Dustin.

By the time I was clean and dressed, there was someone knocking on my door. I went downstairs and opened it to find my old high school boyfriend, Danny.

Danny smiled. I smiled back.

"Hi, Maryellen."

"Danny. How's tricks?"

"Well, you know, I'm in town to visit my brother and my new niece. He had a girl this time."

"How is good ol' Earlybird?" I said.

We used to call Danny's baby brother Earlybird Earl because he was a known fussbudget who'd rather lose a limb than show up at church or school any less than fifteen minutes early. His mother used to say that Earl would make sure to be dead and resurrected twice before anyone else even knew the Rapture had started.

"He's more boring than watching grass grow. Say, I was wondering if you—"

"I'll get my purse."

This was a semi-regular thing. When Danny came back to town, we went out carousing. After trolling roadhouses, we returned to my place to, as I've heard it put, "Netflix and chill."

I was out the door not a minute later. The grapefruit-sized egg still hung on my wall hook, momentarily forgotten through the call of my lust.

———

MY FRIEND JACKIE DROPPED US BACK OFF AT HOME, THREE sheets to the wind, too blitzed to steer the ship but too old to be stupid enough to drunk drive either.

Some call that wisdom.

Me and Danny stood under the fading yellow porch light as it projected the shadows of moths' aerial maneuvers. Danny kept grabbing at me (not in a bad way). I needed to concentrate because the lock kept moving away from my key.

"Maryellen, I—you know, I like—I—"

I turned around and held my finger to my lips, trying

not to laugh, "Shhhh. I got neighbors. They're late when it sleeps. I mean—Danny, hey, Danny—what do I mean?"

"You mean they're sleeping when you—" Danny stumbled back into my wind chime and made it jangle "—shit!"

I started laughing hysterically. Through catching my breath, I managed to tell Danny that I thought my neighbors probably shat during daylight hours, too. He didn't get it. To be fair, I'm not sure it was a joke.

I got the key in the lock and opened the door. Danny grabbed my wrist and stopped me from walking in.

"Hold on, little lady. It's late at night and the light's not bright. Lemme check your homestead," he said and waggled his eyebrows.

I laughed and held one arm toward my door like a girl presenting game show prizes. "My hero. You're chivalrous as shit."

Danny walked inside. A few steps in, he abruptly stopped. I heard a gurgling sound. Then a croaking sound, like when you're in really bad pain but don't have the wind to cry out. Danny just stood there, spasmodically shaking.

"Danny, what are you doing?" I reached inside and to the left of him and switched on the vestibule light.

I saw why Danny was stock-still and gurgling. Two foot-and-a-half-long barbs punctured his neck and the side of his head at his temple, respectively. There came a thick, quick slushing sound as the barbs slickly slid out of his throat and skull. Danny convulsed as he fell to the floor. I stared, unable to move.

A half-dozen legs, each like a seven-foot-long bendable stilt, carried forward a massive head the size of a yoga ball. My adrenal glands secreted enough to quickly boot me off my drunk.

I put together the sequence in my head: the first egg

gave birth to the first tiny head with legs; the first tiny head with legs gave birth to the bigger egg; the bigger egg gave birth to this.

The barbs snapped back into the egg-shaped-head's mouth. The thing's six legs locomoted like a basketball-hoop-high spider crab's. Its height was all long limbs.

I screamed. I turned to run. It snared me on one of its crustacean spindles. The appendage was no thicker than a garden hose, but the kinetic strength of the other five legs produced an unimpedible force as the six-legged-head flung me like a ragdoll across my living room.

I hit headfirst into a wall. Everything went black.

———

I WOKE UP IN THE CORNER OF MY LIVING ROOM. THE SIX-legged-head was much bigger than before. A proboscis like a livid blood-red bamboo chute extended from the middle of its forehead, down to the ground, where it had punctured Danny's body through the top of his skull. I heard slurping and sucking noises over a sound like a wet/dry shop vacuum.

As it sucked out Danny's brains and guts, the six-legged-head metamorphosed. Bulbs of flesh molded on its face. Bones broke and reset to altered curvatures. It was a nightmare claymation, a freakish Rob Bottin practical effect.

Its face was turning into Danny's.

By the time it slurped up all of Danny's insides, the egg's face had completely changed into his. Its proboscis shucked itself free of the swollen puncture in Danny's skull. My date's dead body was shrunken, drained of its every wet drop.

The six-legged-head noticed me, as if I'd only just

appeared. It approached my corner in the gait of a mutated hexapod. Once beside me, it looked down. I looked and saw the top of its head almost touching the ceiling tiles.

"I from KCGA." The six-legged-head spoke in Danny's voice. I started crying. "Neighborly is giving eggs. You happiness with eggs. You loving eggs?"

I covered my mouth to blunt hiccuping sobs, trying not to make noise. It was right there. God, that thing was right there. And Danny's voice…

"I—I—" My voice coming from my body startled me. I was flooded. Had the six-legged-head penetrated my flesh—had it infected my brain? Was I a host dreaming my parasite's dreams?

It chittered and got louder. Under Danny's voice was a noisy, burbling sludge like food through a gassy gut. "You are happiness inside eggs. Are neighboring? HAPPY EGGS?"

"Yes. Yes, I am very happy with the eggs," I managed while bearing down on my weeping.

The six-legged-head seemed to think this over for a minute. It spoke: "Eggs is community. Eggs is neighbors and neighborly. Eggs is friendly and are gooding. You will to buying more eggs?"

"Yes. Yes, I'll buy more eggs, I swear." I looked around for my purse. Did I have cash? Is that what it wanted? I could go to the… (Oh. Oh!) I thought of something. "I just —I have to go to the bank to get money to pay you," I said.

The six-legged-head was processing this. As it worked out my proposal, it spoke its thoughts aloud, "Bank are money. Money are giving KCGA. KCGA god of peoples. Eggs is KCGA. Money is going to for eggs. Ex-ch—ex-ch—ex-ch—"

"Exchange?" I said.

The six-legged-head blew dumb forced laughter out its mouth, like a grade-schooler guffawing at a joke about political economy. Its laughter stopped suddenly enough to almost be violent. "Eggs are money exchange. Eggs is money, are money is KCGA. Money is god of peoples." It leaned over me with a stupid but penetrating gaze.

"Bank are where?"

I pointed toward the door. "In town."

"Money are bank?"

I nodded. "Yes. The money is in the bank."

It bent one of its spidery legs and scratched the neckless underside of its head-body. I don't know if it was thinking or aping a gesture it had seen a thinking creature make. "You go bank?" it said.

"Yes. I go bank."

It skittered backward a few steps and opened a clear path toward the front door, then turned to look back at me. "Eggs is money and are KCGA, god of all peoples. You are going to bank."

I didn't know what it wanted me to do. I didn't move.

"GO," the head said, with much more loudness and force.

I didn't need any more prompting than that. I got to my feet, careful to make no sudden movements. I tip-toed passed the six-legged-head with as wide a berth as I could give.

As soon as I was at my door, I ran.

———

WHEN I CAME BACK WITH THE POLICE, THERE WAS NO evidence any of the things I claimed had happened had actually happened. There was no blood on my living room carpet, no six-legged-head, no egg carton in the trash from the KCGA. No Danny's body. Nothing; all of it, gone.

I was warned that I needed to cut back on the sauce. EMS came and checked me out, asked me how many quarters make up a dollar and who the President was. They said that I might've been soused, but was still plenty lucid.

One of the EMTs nodded his head at me sideways while talking to one of the cops.

The cop came over and asked me a bunch of questions. They were all roundabout, secondary queries. What he was really asking was: Are you now, or have you ever been, a drunken lunatic spinster?

The cop decided the answer was probably yes; I was cited for the misdemeanor crime False Alarm or Report.

I sought psychological counseling—you tend not to believe your own eyes when something happens like what I've precedingly described. I thought it couldn't hurt.

After a week or so, I got a call from Earl asking if I'd seen Danny. I told him we'd gone out, and I told him that I told the cops, too. And I left it at that.

When Earl sees me in the grocery store now, he gets a look on his face like he's smelling shit. Then he turns and walks the other way. I wouldn't be surprised if he wanted to kill me.

———

A MONTH LATER, THERE WAS A CARTON OF EGGS WAITING ON my doorstep when I got home from work. There was a note tied to the carton, knotted to it with twine:

"Enjoy the latest batch. Please remit payment at your convenience.

"Your Friends at the KCGA"

A VIXENLY HEXER

A harlequin Great Dane, black and merle patching its white coat. Stiff, erectile ears, cropped on a concrete block head. Eyes tired but no less hungry for that. The size. Big, even for the breed. You could confuse it for a Pinzgauer cattle, burly baby-tree-trunk legs, neck like a horse. Its jaw deformed, mandible bulldoggedly obtruding. Bony shiv teeth too menacing for dog runs built close to jungle gyms.

The man was as naked as the dog. His flesh billowed, an adipose life preserver ringing his torso. Waterlogged leather wallet skin. Nearly scalped, pearlescent green rounding his head in a suppurating King Shit's royal crown. A mesmerizing gynecomastia—one breast hitting the other before the other swung back and did the same. Like a Newton's pendulum.

The man muttered, and if it was a word, it wasn't a nice one. Calves, penis, thighs, smeared with dirt packed with pebbles and roots. He spit out a tooth, hitting the harlequin Dane square in the eye. The dog yelped before lunging at its laughing enemy.

The animal speared the man—a torpedo hit straight to the gut. The fat man gripped the dog's ears and rolled, the two of them a tumbleweed of paws, tongue, fingers, belly, tail. Teeth found purchase in the man's drooping breast. And did he ever howl.

"I'll put it to your mother!"

Maybe the Dane understood that bit before biting down

harder. The man's teeth snapped in the air, too, cranking the dog's head in a guillotine hold.

"I got you this time, you shitter," he said, almost intimately. "I've got you this time."

Two women on a gingham blanket sat atop the small hill; sat, as it were, ringside for the bout. One with her legs stuck out in front of her, like a doll plopped on a wall shelf. Head through a ponchoed black rag, front and back flaps tethered with rope. The tattered garment's boxy shape was inelegant, but revealing, like a side-slit dress, her skin bronzed from days of long hours naked in the sun. A vixenly hexer. "Witch," had been said.

The other woman sat knees-up with her elbows propped on them. A stranger hiking her way through to her cousin's head shop in Colorado. Her hair hung in frazzled twin braids the color of candy bars and the texture of boiled wool. She prodigiously sucked her vape, nostrils two steaming pots. Her septum bullring carved Os from the vapor; neat trick, whether she was trying for it or not.

"How long do you let them go for?" the stranger asked.

The hexer rolled her eyes up in her head in search of an answer, a hum rumbling from her throat to her tongue. "Depends who's done worse. If Ted's actin' up worse, I keep 'em goin'. 'Cause Ted don't quit till he's dead. But the man ain't got the wind—"

The stranger offered her vape.

"No thanks," the hexer shook her head. "—but if Ratchet forgets hisself—say, goes nosin' in my flower bed—"

"I love flowers. I just about died seeing the botanical gardens."

Jaws opened, sun silhouetting them the shape of a grappler-bucketed backhoe. Dogteeth sunk forearm flesh, the man kicking his fat legs out at the Dane's. Stuck behind the eight ball, feet too far past the dog's forelegs, neither the hindlimbs close enough.

"Coral bells and daylily. I grow 'em myself," she said, smiling with pride. "—then I keep it to short rounds, so Ted gets in his licks, 'fore Ratchet's warmed up. Ratchet gets all stymied. 'Bloodlust's blue balls,' mama called it. Pig-ignorant thing to say, maybe. She ain't had no school. Saying stuck, anyhow."

"Bloodballs?" The stranger offered with a smile, a life-long student in her four older brothers' juvenility master class. She pulled two beers from her backpack, held one out.

"No thanks," the hexer said. She chuckled. "—bloodballs. Why, yes, I suppose it'd be just that."

The stranger popped the tab on one and stuck the other tallboy back in her bag.

Ratchet's jaw crocodile-locked Ted's wrist, twisting, yanking; a chunk of flesh tore away, the radial artery ruptured. Ted's water-bagged eyes dimmed as blood geysered from his wrist. He threw wild punches while his lips ran pale; flailing, nothing connecting, a whole man weaker every time he swung.

"Does it work?" The stranger eyed her host while sipping her beer.

"Well," the hexer said, musing, "my mama always told me—she says, 'Baby, you can kill 'em with kindness, but you're better off just killin' 'em with killin' 'em till they learn.'" The hexer let out a whoop. "Go 'head an' look now," she said, cocking her chin back towards the scrap, "Ratchet's got him good."

Ratchet nudged past Ted's depleted guard and began to eat his throat. Both hexer and stranger spectated as impassively as if sitting in lawn chairs watching the last stragglers in a charity walk. Ratchet consumed Ted's throat to the last.

Once it was over, the hexer stood up. She hocked something up her throat, spat it out her gullet: a fire-tailed pink meteor. It landed in Ted's mouth.

Ted's head weeble-wobbled. He gasped a just-Narcanned-junkie's reviving gasp. Managing himself to his knees, his palms bore his weight, belly hung overground.

The hexer got to her feet, arms akimbo and shaking her head. She cupped her hands and yelled down the battleground, "You gonna' quit eatin' that pie off the ledge 'fore I say so, Ted?"

Ted looked up. With some effort, he said, "Yes, dear."

"I sure hope so!" She looped her thumb and forefinger between her lips and blew like yesteryear's New York natives hailing their taxis. Ratchet scurried uphill for mama, harlequin coat spattered gory and red.

The hexer hollered down to her beau:

"Come on then. It's dinnertime. We got company." She turned toward the stranger. "You stayin'?"

Wiping sixteen-ounce suds from her lips, the stranger squinted against the sun. She smiled. "Sure. Why not?"

MEETING IVOR VOËLMAN

I vor Voëlman is a wizard of deep dread, conjuring spookery almost alchemical. Naturally his readers' eyebrows are singed now and again.

Strange things happen when Ivor releases a new book:

After the 2009 reissue of *Mother Tongue*, a Biltmore Hotel maintenance man put a copy in almost all the nearly-seven-hundred rooms' nightstand drawers. That same night in Los Angeles, only a few miles west, twenty-seven girls were born in the same hospital at the exact same time.

When *Gunmetal Ghouls* was published, the Louisianan shipping magnate Lew Pollinger papier-mâchéd his home's whole exterior with dustjackets stripped from thousands of hardback copies. He subsequently experienced a mental breakdown attempting to buy every distributor in America that had ever sold Voëlman's books, the details of which were written up in the *New York Post* exposé, "Pollinger Nuts for Novels!"

Let those benign eccentricities of Voëlman fandom not obscure his diehards' severer derangements. Few familiar with Ivor Voëlman will have forgotten the morbid case of Inez Abreu, who jumped off the Millenium BCP bank headquarters in Porto, while Rádio e Televisão de Portugal's local affiliate broadcast her death. The police negotiator was within ten feet of Abreu when she jumped, at which moment he swore to have heard her say: *"Diga a eles que eu morri por Voëlman."* ("Tell them I died for Voëlman.")

My own minor fixation went no further than dressing up as Mr. Clip from *Headhunters*: peak-lapeled black-and-red pinstripe over a necktie greasy with deep-crimson gore. That, my Halloween costume between the ages of twelve and too-old-to-trick-or-treat.

Oh, how Ivor's stories can so fry his readers' brains. And when I read Ivor Voëlman, something cooks inside me, too.

It's more than suspending my disbelief. I choke on raging fire's toxic smoke between chapter heads, taste spilt blood on the pages, hear poltergeists rattling chains between the book boards; sensory intoxication by bone, blood, and smoke. Briefly, I become his characters; the hophead chased through Victorian public houses and opium dens, and the Red Fiend at his heels; the unhinged experimenter mutating his avenging golem, and the perpetrators of pogroms to whom, at last, his vengeance comes. I enter a thralldom of true fear populated by flesh-eating ghouls.

I was more than a fan of Ivor Voëlman. I was a part of him.

———

A HAND RAPPED MY FRONT DOOR HARD ENOUGH TO SERVE A warrant. I heard my cat, Barge, yowl and knock over my toothbrush cup set on the upstairs bathroom sink; the cup chimed, cracked and crunched, and had certainly broke. Sometimes Barge decapitated mice and left their bodies for me to find. But she was never around. I never saw her at all, really.

I went to open the door.

Zola was standing on my stoop under an eclipse of

moths throwing themselves in woozy circles under a flickering bulb. Tautened legs and high cheekbones and coffee-colored skin. Eyes that gleamed the lustrous honeyed chocolate of tiger's eye stones. Zola told me many mutually-contradicting personal histories, her life retold in revisions and drafts. I am sure every version is true.

Why had she come? Even while we'd hunted the death-cultists who'd burnt her voodooist botanica to cinders, Zola had never visited my home.

"Zola…" I closed the door behind me except for a small crack. "What are you doing here?"

"I need to show you something. Can I come inside?" She looked up at the moths. Why she then blew at them hard enough to send them to a tailspin, I can't say.

I looked over my shoulder at my door. There were chunks gouged out of the doorjamb and a permanent black streak from the medical reseller removing my mother's hospital bed.

"I…" Her slender fingers touched my forearm. "I don't care." I turned back to find her body nearer mine, skin effusing aromas of cosmetics and perfume. Zola's canines gleamed, wolf's teeth touched up by an ultrasonic scaler.

"Give me one second," I said.

"Take all the time you need."

Except I heard her closing the front door behind her two seconds after I went inside. Zola eyed the club chair in the living room corner. She went and ran her hand over its olefin fabric. Her fingernails scraped and caught on pilled bumps along the chair.

When my mother entered the purgatory of full incontinence but only partial bedriddenness, she'd piss there, in her favorite seat. That she continued wallowing in that chair, even while soaked in her piddle, showed, I suppose, that her preferences never changed. I'd dumped industrial cleaner in quantities satisfactory for chemical warfare to cover up the stink. It nevertheless lingered in my memory's unscrubbable corners.

The invisible fog of my mother's decay smothered me. I don't know why I kept her chair.

I looked up and saw the moths' eclipse; they'd followed from my stoop to orbit the bowl lamp on the living room ceiling. They barrel-rolled and dipped exactly the same as before, their flight patterns identical. It was not déjà vu so much as bit-for-bit transposition.

Zola puffed air at the moths again. I held my breath as she blew. An inexplicable anxiety stole over me, akin to that of watching someone holding a flaming book of matches next to a gasoline pump.

"Can I sit down?" she said.

I didn't want her to sit in the club chair. "I'm sorry, I— it's been a long time since I had anyone over." But I didn't object.

"It's okay." She fell into the battered chair. I thought of my mother's ghost's excretions. If Zola smelled anything, though, she kept her poker face about it.

I contemplated Mom's old shag rug; its cigarette burns and bald spots. I remembered renting a Rug Doctor from Home Depot before the wake. Or maybe that wasn't a memory. Maybe it was an idea I'd had.

Zola's polychrome eyes flashed over her seat. "It's okay," she said. Her voice, a cigarette-addict's and a sexpot's, sultry but blown out, raspy. Zola acted how I imagined a fox playing dead to catch a rabbit acting. "I got to show you something."

My neck drew up hackles. "Okay," I said.

She sucked her teeth, eyes rolling in her head. "It's not

if I should show you, but I got to show you. There's a difference, right?"

"Sure."

"Here. Here, look at this." Zola reached into her
shoulder bag and pulled out a clothbound hardback book,
its buckram sun-bleached a weathered dark-denim blue. At
the top of the front cover was gilt-stamped the title,
Whispers, with the foil faded the color of tarnished brass. On
the bottom, also in gold, was written: "all best, Fritz".

She handed it to me.

I knew exactly what book this was.

Whispers was a horror magazine founded amidst the
genre's nineteen-seventies boom. The "Fritz" in question
was Fritz Leiber, a well-known speculative fiction author
who'd first made his bones in the pre-war pulps.

That hardback edition of *Whispers* (Vol. 4, No. 1-2), a
copy of which I now held in my hand, was a special Leiber
double-issue. Only two-hundred-fifty copies were ever
printed. A rumor had been bruited about, that one of those
two-hundred-fifty copies had a hidden insert between the
flyleaves. On that insert was reputedly written a phone
number. And if you called that number...

It's an odd sensation feeling your throat constrict while
your lungs are desperate for air. "Is it...?" My hands were
shaking.

"I know you've been looking for it," Zola said.

As I held the hardback open, Zola started thumbing
through it. She turned to a page bookmarked with a lime-
green slip of paper. I stared at the slip. A phone number was
scrawled on it in the black ink of a fountain pen.

Time narrowed, then dilated. A potent irreality wrung
my senses right out.

"Maybe you should call," I said. An instinct of self-preservation, for which reason could not account, forbade me dialing the number. "Or maybe…" neither of us should call, I thought.

Zola's face turned up a question mark. "But what if you have to be the caller to win the prize?"

"What prize?"

Zola shrugged.

I dialed my cellphone and waited. There was no ringtone, but a breathy shiver. A sequence of wet clicks, followed by crackling distortion. A quiet weeper gloomily trilling her lips, perhaps; a paraphiliac hyperventilating? It was haunting—violative. Violative in the way of a trussed-up sexual masochist loitering near a seesaw.

The receiver clicked. A steady respiration hummed along the phone line's static rhythm. A man's voice, articulating in baritone, cut crystal clear across the line:

"'It is good to be a cynic—it is better to be a contented cat—'"

The spook trailed off to silence. Dead air.

I spent a half-minute thinking as a ghostly mains hum held the line.

"'And it is best not to exist at all'," I finally said.

(Maybe) I heard a brief, low laugh. But the dial tone's abrupt drone cut the call. I put my cellphone on the floor and stared at it.

Whereupon someone slowly knocked at my front door.

———

We locked eyes before both turning toward the door.

I stood up. Zola's little fingers slipped fumbling for my

wrist. I stepped to my front door, white-knuckling while I twisted the knob. I stopped.

"Don't," Zola said.

Time shrank and swelled again. I edged along a world-steep precipice.

I opened the door and I pushed the door all the way open.

There was no one there. I stepped outside the door. There was no one around.

I looked down and saw an envelope left on the doormat.

I picked it up and brought it back inside, closing the door behind me.

"What was it?" Zola said.

I held up the envelope.

Zola's shoulders relaxed, eyes and lips loosening. "Oh…" She studied me studying the mail. "Are you going to open it?" she said.

"Maybe you should."

"Why?"

"Okay, I'll open it."

She slipped past and plucked the envelope from my fingers. "I don't mind." Zola ran her acrylic thumbnail under the seal flap. (An open envelope, to me, looks like a broken-mouthed cartoon.) Out came a folded typewritten letter. I saw intendedness in the tight twist of Zola's face as she read.

"What is it?"

Zola shushed me. "I'm reading it now."

The perforated thermal paper of airline boarding passes peeked out of the envelope. There was a separate piece of linen cardstock on which was printed flawless, calligraphic handwriting, with ornamental letterhead at the top. I grabbed for the fancy cardstock; Zola slapped my hand.

"Stop. You're just making me go slower." I tried to look closer; she elbowed me away.

Presently Zola smiled. "It's an invitation."

"An invitation?"

"From Ivor Voëlman."

"It's an invitation…from Ivor Voëlman."

"We're booked on a first-class flight tomorrow." She handed the envelope over to me.

"We?" I'd thought right; they were boarding passes. One with Zola's name.

"I'm going to stay here tonight. If that's alright."

Zola walked away and up the stairs. She disappeared up the unlit upper floor. Her blouse floated down from the higher dark and landed on the handrail. Her strapless bra fluttered after, a butterfly with rounded wings.

I followed.

So proceeded the series of unreal events that would permanently alter my existence.

———

In first class they use ice tongs to hand you hot towels rolled into thumblike buns, steam still coming off them. A man sitting opposite us wiped his face with his towel, so I wiped my face with mine, too. Mine smelled of the decomposing lignin in old paper. Despite it, the hot towel felt nice. The way the air felt cold on my face after I used it felt nice.

I stared out the porthole, caught sight of a coal-black cloud in the sky—a trick of the light, a smudge on the window. It had wings.

Zola drank three vodka sodas and passed out somewhere off the coast of Savannah. She drooled an inky iron gall from the corner of her mouth. I touched it. I rubbed it between my thumb and fingers. It wetly crumbled. I brought it up to my nose, smelling copper, ammonia.

I would've asked the flight attendant for a fresh towel to wipe off my hand, but before she drifted back down the aisle my fingers became spotlessly clean. I did a double-take on Zola, saw her mouth breathing sleep through unstained lips.

The flight attendant who later passed by was different from the last. Every flight attendant that passed by was different. I never saw the same one twice.

———

I'D NEVER BEEN TO PALM BEACH BEFORE. IN FACT, BEFORE Zola and I tangled with the cultists, necessitating our Flatbush, Brooklyn escapade, I had never left Pennsylvania.

The Billows was an Americanized Galleria Borghese; loggias and bell towers, a quarry's-worth of Indiana limestone shoring up a thousandfold fenestration of architraved windows, the full complement of Renaissance Revival architecture besides.

It made a red-headed stepchild of Mar-a-Lago.

We cruised a racecourse-long drive laid with red clay pavers enough to empty a brickworks, more palm trees than I'd ever seen in my whole life. A halogen-lit fountain accommodated marbled fauns and cherubs whose charge was to keep those experiencing the symptoms of poverty at bay.

The driver, wearing sunglasses with lenses faintly tinted rose-pink, regarded me through his rearview mirror. There was something wrong with his eyes that the lenses obscured.

"You nervous?" He was dressed in a once-black two-piece suit bled gray from wear. I imagined him a frail and careworn human-shaped crow.

"Terrified," I said.

"Ain't no need. He wants you how you are. Wants us all the way we are. To see the deep insides of us. Root deep down in our guts."

He plucked his tongue in his cheek. Then, rubbed his belly in an obscene parody of a pregnant woman. What followed was a short but enthusiastic sequence of pelvic thrusts directed toward the windshield.

"You feel you got strings goes to your guts? I got strings goes to my guts. Anatomy's a grim destiny. Strips us to our uncooked fate! Raw. Raw, raw, raw. That's how bossman likes it. Get inside the puppet's meat." His sunglasses slid down his nose. Chemiluminescent egg yolks were glopped inside his eye sockets. "Ain't no shame being a marionette! Good to got strings goes inside your deep meats. Yessirree!"

"Are we…" The world outside my window spun in the wonky revolutions of a damaged zoetrope. "Are we close?"

"Do you know the first thing you do when you field dress a deer?" He snortled, rubbed his forefinger's middle knuckle underside of his nose. "You remove the sex organs. Lust leaves a stink, is the problem. It leaves a stink. You ever think about that? How it leaves a stink? You got to sterilize the meat so it ain't stanken! Tell a story in flesh, it's gotta be fresh. Gotta be fresh! *Tablet rascal.* That's Latin for 'blank plate'. The Brothers Grimm ain't never wrote on no scribbly looseleaf!"

The driver winked at Zola through the rearview. Zola giggled like a pullstring doll who someone had yanked her cord.

"Ivor is flesh and blood. Just like you and me, boy. 'For the life of the flesh is in the blood!' You see this? Look,

look." The driver pinched and pulled his right cheek so hard I could hear it. "Flesh and blood, boy, flesh and blood. We're the language of meat, son! Speak in these tongues!"

"Don't do that. Please!" I stretched from the backseat to stop him contusing his face. But my stomach curdled itself seasick the very moment I leaned in, put on the verge of a chundering heave.

I slumped back until the feeling passed.

"Take the membrane out the beast," our chauffeur raved along, "so's it gets plucked, so's it gets tanned; slicing and dicing parchment slivers out the sheepskin; rip the vellum out of baby-pure calves. Dermatopilectomy—that's what they call it!"

He broke out in goonish laughter. Tears runnelled his eyes' wrinkled corners, face ruddling a rheumatic-fever-red. He cackled till he was wheezing, then coughed his tongue outside of his mouth.

His mania at last came to softly simmer. Once recomposed, the driver spoke again in a hush: "Did I tell you the first thing you do when you field dress a deer?"

I turned to gauge Zola's reaction. She seemed not to have heard anything at all. I turned back toward the front. There was a rosy bruise rising on the driver's right jowl. He watched the road as if he'd just been silent for hours, days, his blighted eyes hidden again under the rose-pink tints.

We continued up the brick drive.

I CAUGHT THE SCENT OF A STERILELY-SEASALTED COASTLINE, an over-purified sea lapping the over-purified sand of an over-purified shore. A zone of inoculation—against strays' leftover dogshit and the sun-scalded ballpark dogs kids never finish eating and the yeasty-sweet stink of crushed beer cans —against public beaches' whole rancid fundament. These grounds abided a mercenary tidiness.

Bounded within this pristine-green aesthetic was the unexpected pungency of cycads' rotten-fruit reek.

The boots of the palms' bark were saw-toothed with sharp spines. A gardener in a white banded-collar shirt trimmed the flora so close that a syrupy guck wept from the over-clipped fronds; another wielded a backpack sprayer full of herbicide to exterminate garden pests in the flowerbeds and turf. The resort's landscaping was a symbol of both classism's ruthless sterility and its inequity's irrepressible ooze and funk.

Very pretty, though.

———

WE CAME TO A PORTE-COCHÈRE FOR HOTEL GUESTS' disembarkation into the shade, a balustraded terrace built above it, where on the railing sat several monstrous black birds. Birds bigger than albatross, with hypno-discoid yellow eyes. A parliament of striges, infant-devourers from metamorphoses of Greek myth; brimful of bloodthirst, talons barbed and bent. I felt a powerful urge to urinate.

Under the porte-cochère were the ceiling-height doors of The Billows' grand entrance. Ivor Voëlman stood at the fore.

I wondered how long he had been there waiting for me.

———

"MR. HURSTON! *WELKOM BY JOU HUIS, MY LIEWE SEUN!* Truly, it is a great pleasure for me to see you." Accent much sharper than in his interviews, his Afrikaner cadence reeled between trilled Rs and unaspirated stops. "I am grateful of your choosing to accept my invitation. I hope there is a sense, to you, of returning home. *Maar ek is klaar geskryf, en nou is jy hier. Dis omtrent tyd.*"

A strix stood a stone's throw just behind Voëlman, at where the porte-cochère's shade touched the drive's sunbeat brick; not flown, I thought, but vanished from the terrace to rematerialize on the ground. It was as a revenant palpably seething within a taxidermy mount, fever boiling the wood wool and rags inside the preserved skin of the specimen.

The bird's face was bald and bruised in the same spot as the driver's. I gave a once-over the roadway and found our chauffeur disappeared.

My first impression of Ivor Voëlman was of but a slip of a man. But his limbs drew longer as he moved closer, stretching his frame to two heads taller than mine.

A sudden sunshower wetted the pavement. The smell of petrichor rose up from the ground as the sky shaded the gray of effloresced concrete.

Zola walked after a trolley stacked with our luggage, carted by a man in plain sight who was unable to be seen.

———

We STRODE A HAND-TUFTED CARPET OF FLORID BUT sufficiently understated design to satisfy the staid preferences of old money. Further ahead, the elevator's brass hoistway doors swallowed Zola sideways, eating her up along with the trolley and porter. She ran her tongue under the points of her eyeteeth as the elevator doors closed. I was dubious of her mouth's ability to contain such sharp canines.

"*Alles is goed en alles sal goed wees.* Your friend Zola, I promise, is receiving royal treatment." Voëlman enfolded my far shoulder in his lengthy fingers' grasp, hooking my neck in the crook of his elbow. "You have questions, I am sure. You must have questions."

"Are you really Ivor Voëlman?"

He laughed loud and raucous and pulled me tight into his side. "You would not be here now if I were not Ivor Voëlman. Whyever should I tell you I am someone I am not? *Waansin!*"

I delicately nodded, as if an animate, crystalline figurine for whom too much movement would shatter. My host, perhaps sensing my seeming frailty, projected a demonstrable earnestness when he said, "I am Ivor Voëlman. Do we understand one another?"

My eyes stung wetly. I squeezed them shut tight. "Thank you."

———

SMALL CATASTROPHES WERE COMMON JUST BEFORE MY mother's death. I remember, once, she scraped her paper-thin skin against a jagged coffee table corner. A red canyon opened across her outer thigh, the gorge of a wound filling with blood. I watched, helpless, too far away to catch her, as she twisted and stumbled. Watched her fall over, watched her body smack into the floor so hard that she rattled the joists. The ground gave no give; she didn't bounce at all.

She bled rivers of blood her body couldn't spare. By then she was already demented. And so she cried in demented incomprehension as she smeared blood all over herself. She dementedly tantrumed and fled from me in horror. It is not uncommon for a demented mother to forget her son's face along with his name.

I now stood shoulder to shoulder with Voëlman, and my mother would never know it.

That there are more bad things than good things—that, I can accept. What bothers me is the cruelty of the timetable.

I tried to think of my mother's face, but I could not. I tried to think of her name, but I could not. It's a curious thing, memory disappearing while the lost memory's pain carries over.

But for all that, here I was.

"Thank you," I said again.

Ivor put his hands on my shoulders. His eyes bored deep in mine. "You are in the right place." He patted my cheek with his hand. "Good man, good man."

We paced the stately gaud that echoed the Gilded Age's twilight, encountering neither blue-blooded guests nor blue-collared staff. Through a flatbed-sized window I saw the ocean in turmoil but couldn't hear its rushing tide. What I heard were nails clawing at desiccated wood and a gurgling death rattle somewhere outdoors.

"Where is everybody?"

"This way, this way," Ivor said, waving me to follow. "Come, come, Dennis, come. Follow me—*vinnig, vinnig*—through here. Follow me."

We entered a domed room nearly three stories high, its ceiling frescoed in the style of a Renaissance Revival mural. One might expect to see the patriciate's *nobiluomini e nobil-donne* in their gilt-threaded garments, an Olympian standing contrapposto over awestruck mortals. There were instead raptorial guildsmen more like monsters than men.

Here the striges, strangely dressed as skilled human tradesmen.

Oily-black bodies angrily ruffled behind their prison of

painted wet lime plaster, eyes suppurating an infective neon yellow that dribbled down the fresco. Some dressed as ship-wrights wielding caulking mallets, some plowmen holding sickles or flails, others barber-surgeons clutching straight razors and strops. A thick crust coated their instruments, turning their hammers, razors, and hooks a dried dark-red. It stained their doublets; speckled their *camicie* and their ruffled cuffs.

Light came through the glass oculus at the dome's apex, kaleidoscopically gloaming over the rotunda. A gray sky, spotted with the dark purple of day-old bruises. The rounded room's aroma hinted at spilled, now-spoiled blood.

"What are they?" I pointed up at the ceiling, the striges laughing deep in their chests. They riffled feathers about their quaking bodies, releasing from their preen glands a putrefactive musk.

"Who?"

The winged guildsmen's talons shimmered iridescent as oil slick. I kept pointing. "Them."

Ivor's bassy laugh climbed out from deep in his belly. "Oh, they're very special. Very, very special. *Die skepsels van my hart. Die skeppers!*"

Standing at the further of a lone table's two place settings, Ivor gripped the crest rail at the top of his side's undrawn chair. Moving his chairback grip, his fingers dripped the same inky iron gall earlier seeped from Zola's sleeping lips, wet-black fingerprints smearing the satin brocade. Lightning struck above the oculus, lighting up the sky's bruisy gloom, flooding the dome and turning the room the color of trapped blood.

"Sit, sit," Ivor said, holding one hand palm-up toward the chair opposite his.

Nothing in the preceding days unnerved me as being

asked to sit down at that table did. There was a threat of finality to it—as if sitting with a harbinger so we'd count my ill omens.

The convex ceiling slouched towards us, while the striges, their beaks deformed in denticulated grins, slowly peeled away from their brushmarked plane into three-dimensional being; intending, it seemed, to menace me.

Iron gall ran down the wall, curdling once at the bottom into a jelly that looked and smelled like gore. "Sit," Ivor said. "Sit, Dennis, Sit."

Striges spiraled groundward in helical strakes, skulking through the discharge sliding down the dome's crown, creeping through their own shadows which, with gall and oily-black feathers, emulsified into a living black mortar that washed over the cylindered wall.

Their bodies writhed, tectonically convulsing, shaking the rotunda.

I sat across from Voëlman, paralyzed in the tonic immobility of dumbstruck prey, hands glued to the table and back stuck to my seat.

Ivor sat down, too.

Everything became so impossibly still that it may as well all have been statuary and painted scenery. There remained only the faint drone that fills sound's absence.

Until he spoke.

"Why are you here, Dennis?"

"I don't know."

Ivor pulled deep through his nose before exhaling an air of regret. "But you do, Dennis. You do. Why are you here?"

"I don't know."

Ivor frowned.

The knives, forks, and spoons of his place setting pixelated in patchy electric snowfall, resembling graphic bits fragmentarily misfiring in a video game on the fritz.

The glitching silverware became a full set of fountain pens.

"Do not be difficult." Ivor sneered as he spoke, bobbling his unhappy head. "You are, all of you, always so difficult. But there is nowhere for you to go and nothing else to do. *Verstaan*, this is the terminal through which all my creations must pass. Do you not understand?" He pressed the bridge of his nose between his thumb and two fingers, shook his head while closing his eyes. "I know you know why you are here. Tell me so yourself."

An intolerable proposition confronted me. But I could not credit such an unspeakable thought, let alone speak it aloud. Trembling, I feebly answered: "I—I really don't know."

I wouldn't have believed the speed and brutality with which Ivor then moved his right hand if I hadn't seen it myself.

He drove the arrowheaded nib of the fountain pen through the meat between my knuckles, spearing my left hand all the way through to the table. I screamed with an animal howl begun in my hindbrain.

I bucked against my skewer, but I'd been mounted to the tabletop. The pain was supernatural.

At the last, I rode it out.

Eventually I stopped pulling; eventually I stopped screaming, too. My head nodded backward over my shoulder, as if magnetically repulsed by my skewered hand.

My screams lastly faded as a boiled teakettle quickly cooling.

"Look at your hand, Dennis."

"No," I weakly said.

"Look."

"No."

"*Jou moederfok!* Look, Dennis. Or I will make you look," Ivor said.

I looked. I saw.

Black ink trickled on the tablecloth from in between my knuckles, pooling itself where there ought to have been blood.

"Do you see now?" Ivor said. "Do you?"

"I'm real. I'm real," I said, recognizing but desperate to repudiate the cruelty of my circumstance.

"That is not true. You are what I make you to be—*ek is jou beheerder*: the thing that speaks as my story requires, that must say and do the things for which you are created to do and say."

"I'm real. I'm really real, I know that I'm real, I'm—"

"STOP. Enough, Dennis. Enough."

I sobbed the quiet sobs of a whimpering child retreating from a crying jag. "You can't, you can't finish me, please. There's more. I can be more and you can make it so I'm more…I promise, oh my God, I promise…"

"I have brought you here because it is the end now. *Ons is klaar.* Is that not why you are here? Because we are done?"

"No. No, no, no. No, please. Mom, my mom, please… please, where is my mother?"

"Okay," Ivor said, nodding his head. "Okay, Dennis. Tell me your mother's name, and I will bring her to you. Tell me your mother's name, and you will not be forced to go."

My stunted tongue could not speak the unintelligible phonology sifted from my memory's debris. "Mother" was categorically expurgated. Lost beyond retrieval, if ever there at all.

My body was severed of all impulse, subsiding in my chair.

How? My mother, who I'd seen through the agony of her disintegration, that ought to have scarred me with her name. A wilting vegetable in the husk of her home hospital bed. Her voice, now lost in memories of all the world's other sounds. Her face's shape, of whose barest outline I could no longer trace.

"Because she never had one," Ivor said. "I never gave her one. No face, no name. Like Barge, a cat you own but who you have never seen. *Die verdwynende kat.* And Zola—a voodoo queen persecuted by the shadowy figures of a secret society? *Domkop!* Do such things happen in real life? Her history I wrote and rewrote over until I discovered what suited best. Yes, Zola—*sy nogal iets!* She is a magnificent composition, to sing my own praises."

Zola, I thought. Zola had been here. And maybe she was still here. Maybe she could tell me this was not what it was. "Zola," I said. "Where's Zola?"

"She is gone already. She is already gone," Ivor said. "Zola quite easily reconciled herself to the book of her fate."

What if it was true? What if I…? But, no, here I was; thinking, perseverating, despairing. A fiction cannot be divided by psychological schism. Was it possible I was a figment, a fabricated not-thing? Fractures shot through my glass soul, splintering and spalling into shards and slivers, and then:

I broke. And began again to quietly cry.

"Shh, shh, no, no, no. *Thula baba, thula sana, my seun.* None of that now. None of that. So few are ever ready. And that, I do not expect. I only expect that you should go when it is time." He gently petted my head, then pushed a bent knuckle up under my chin. Our eyes met. "And now, it is time."

"Her name was—her name was—it was—"

Ivor's face turned up a pitying smile. He leaned across the table and gently removed the fountain pen. I felt nothing and saw no scar, no wound, no bleeding. Ivor took my mended hand in both of his.

We were no longer in the dome but standing beside the ocean. Crackling veins of ink and cruor surged across the sky. We were surrounded by the striges, all of them grown two men high. And despite their serrated beaks and hypnotizing yellow eyes, each looked at me through the shape of Ivor Voëlman's face.

"This is it, Dennis. I have no more time to give you. The End. *Die koeël is deur die kerk.*" Ivor touched my face. His hands were warm, eyes warmer. "Yes, the endings are always so very bittersweet."

"If I remember—I just need—"

"Here. Here, here, come here, Dennis." Ivor Voëlman wrapped me in his arms and held me and whispered in my ear, "'But at the last, as every thing hath end/She took her leave, and needs would wend.'" He pulled away and, tendering his regretful smile, firmly grasped my shoulders. "Do you know what that means? *Verstaan?*"

I shook my head.

His smile accounted for the deep sadness of a life whose tragedies had outwritten the consolations of their epilogues. "All good things must come to an end."

In his eyes I saw the reflection of the dome, now in my distant backdrop—saw the reflection of the bruisy firmament above; but I didn't see my own reflection.

"Am I real?" I asked.

"You are realer than most people will ever be. And even

when I die, you will still be who you are. *Wie heuning wil eet, moet steke verdra.* But you will still be who you are."

The sea roiled wild with waves of black ink. At a great distance, a towering fortress stood over a sea fort island. The tower—I saw it clearer now, an obelisk of black dungeons standing athwart the bloody sky—with its spires that pierced the clouds' bellies. Yes, the sea roiled, crashed, and raged. Yet the waters skirting the sea fort prison were as those of tranquil coves hidden behind coral reefs.

In that prison, my peace. Or perhaps, none at all. But understanding? Yes. Yes, that I had found.

"I'm ready," I said.

But I needn't have spoken. The striges had already carried me aloft.

———

OUR LIFE IS QUIET, AND AS THE YEARS PASS SINCE THE publication of *Zola's Maledictions*, and less of Ivor's readers remember our story, our bodies fade and blur. Down the rows of cells, I see the *dramatis personae* of his creation, steadily disappearing. The sinister harridans of *Mother Tongue* are nearly disembodied, bogged flesh and facial features falling away, more sexless mannequins in wet bedsheets than oversexed sisters in too-tight tunics and veils. Mr. Clip's leather tie, once stiffened red with gore, is now a dull russet, his black-and-red pinstripe suit dwindling to transparency with each passing day.

And the rumors that Ivor will soon retire? When that happens, I suppose it won't be very long at all.

We do not eat, excrete, or dream in sleep, or bleed and cry, get sick or tired; but due the prurience of Voëlman's readers, we make love on occasion.

Zola and I wonder which of us will dissipate before the other. As it stands, we seem to go at an even rate. I've been pleasantly surprised at outlasting some very popular characters. I must have been quite the popular character myself.

I wonder if I made many of Voëlman's readers thrill and gasp. I wonder if I made many of them cry. And in my wondering, I wonder, too, at the strangeness of figments harboring their own wretched hopes.

I make a point of listening to all the newcomers' stories. I am still, as I've ever been, an Ivor Voëlman fan.

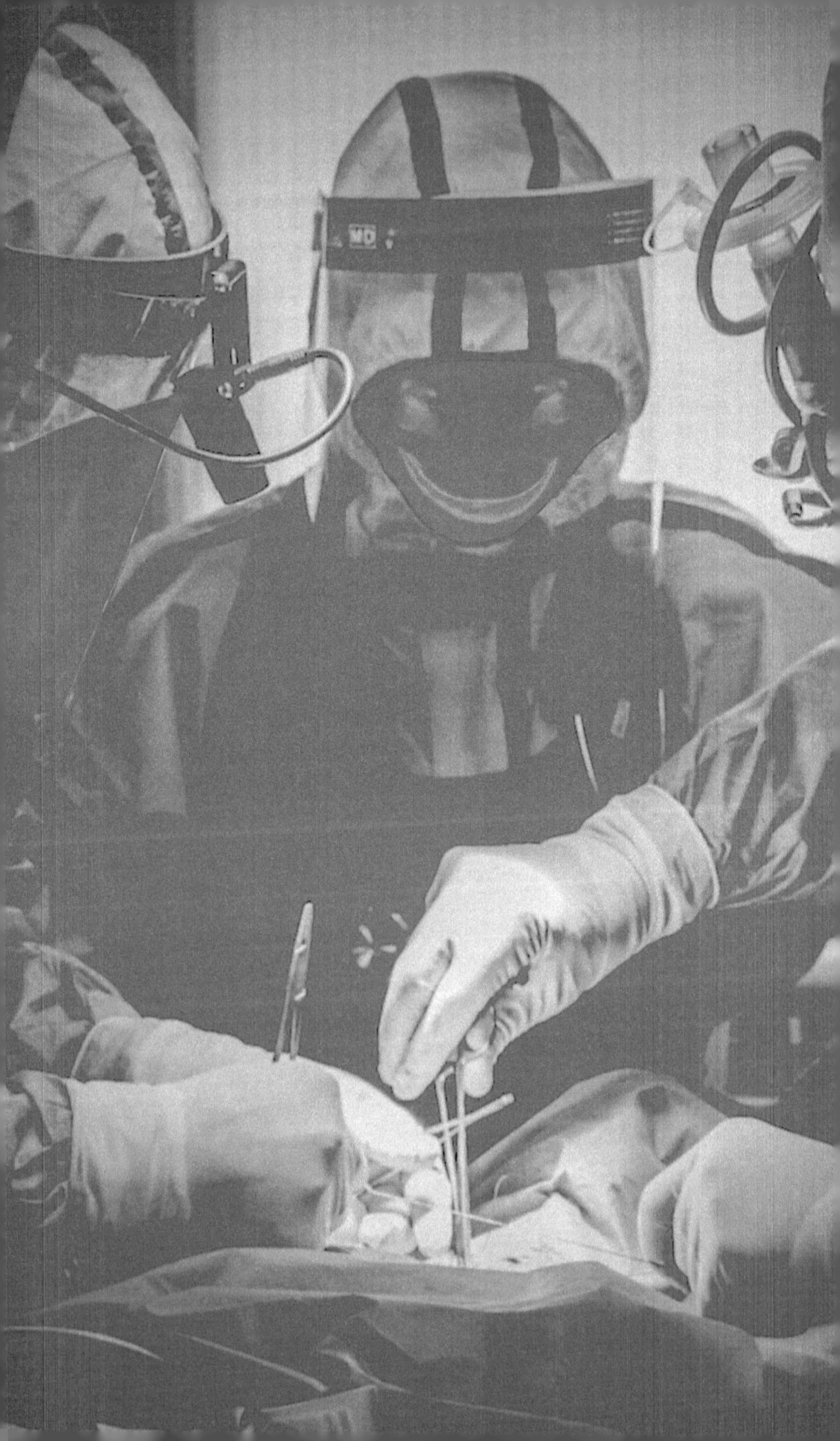

THE EP™ IMPLANT

For years, medical device technology has been unable to keep pace with plastic surgery patients' dynamic needs. Where consumers have sought to surgically enhance their beauty, implantation has been unequal to the task.

Until now.

Enter the revolutionary Esurientem Petat (EP) Implant™: The first-ever Consumer-Adjustable Internal Buttocks Enhancement Device (CAIBED).

With the user-friendly EP App™, implantees can parametrically adjust the contour and buoyancy of their CAIBED, choosing between five preset buttocks shapes: A (Heart), V (Inverted), H (Square), O (Round), and I (Pancake). A companion app, the Caedes Asinorum Fugue™, allows customizable settings in both temperature and weight, and allows users to set their own intervals of creophagous replenishment.

All EP Implants™ include an inbuilt waste vaporizer and calibration port. And the proprietary Rearward Illuminations™ monitoring system allows real-time tracking of changes in size, circulation, enteral nourishment, and flavor.

WARNING: Please ensure that your EP App™ is able to receive daily software updates, and that your smartphone's operating system is fully up-to-date before installation and implantation. Do not open the EP App™ if within ten feet or less of an induction furnace rectifier transformer.

Do not use the EP App™ immediately after eating ice cream, gelato, parfait, mochi, custard, or sorbet.

DO NOT FEED YOUR EP IMPLANT™ AFTER MIDNIGHT.

———

THE PROGRESSION OF LUPITA'S PLASTIC SURGERY ADDICTION had been rather swift. With inherited wealth at hand, she was ushered at speed along the scalpel's Left-Hand Path, regularly indulging her surgical compulsion. Be it breast augmentation with gummy bear implants, extensive otoplasty for her oversized ears, the obligatory nose job, or any of the elective refinements that inevitably followed these procedures (the many that there were), Lupita had done it all.

A radical labiaplasty.

Was it too much? That wasn't really for her to say. Lupita, after all, was a trend-follower, not a trendsetter. The repair of society's sexual complexes (and the self-mutilating proclivity derived therefrom) was beyond her ken.

"I don't understand, though." Lupita was speaking with her physician, Dr. Rezazadeh, inside his Park Avenue office. "I've read every issue of *Plastic and Reconstructive Surgery* since my first mastopexy. There isn't a procedure I haven't heard of. And I'm at the granular level, Rezzie. Not just tits, either. I know the benefits of toe transfer versus finger replantation. I think I ought to have heard of this, too."

"Lupita, my dearest and most favorite patient," Dr. Rezazadeh cooed, ample smarm slickening his salesman's smile, "what the plastic surgery consumer knows and what I tell you are two different things, are they not?"

"Well, yes, I suppose."

Dr. Rezazadeh leaned over his desk, his hands in a basketweave. "The Esurientem Petat costs my patients several hundred-thousand dollars—"

"'Patients'? You mean you've already—"

"—so of course you don't know what it is until I tell you about it. What would be the point of it being marketed to the general public? People who aren't like us—"

But Dr. Rezazadeh caught his political indelicacy in time to course-correct. "What I mean to say is, the average plastic surgery patient doesn't have the resources to consider this procedure. Sometimes, it's better not to know your options if they're not really options you can choose."

"Inequality is so brutal," Lupita said.

"Oh, very much so. I vote the party slate for the Democratic Socialists. Quicker to give a man a fish sandwich than teach him to fish."

"I'm not political. I just want everyone to be happy. As long as you don't hurt anyone doing it, you should do whatever makes you happy."

This sentiment of hers jolted the doctor, his allergy to candor causing him to recede slightly back in his chair.

"Sometimes," she went on, "I think that I ought to give away my money to people who really need it."

Dr. Rezazadeh frowned. "You do?"

"Yes, but then I think that those people will just have to worry about other poor people once they're not the poor ones. I worry so much about poor people, that's what poor people don't realize about being extremely not-poor. I don't want someone else to have to bear that burden."

Dr. Rezazadeh tapped his forefinger to his balding pate, "Heavy is the head that wears the crown. You suffer so others don't have to. Stopping the vicious cycle before it starts. Yes, yes, I quite agree with your tack."

"I give money to PETA, though. They do that whole naked celebrity thing, and I think that's just wonderful. No fatties, either. If animals can be naked all the time, then maybe we should be naked all the time, too. And animals don't own real property, either. Which really throws the homelessness issue into a whole different light. Do you think Jesus had pets?"

"I'm not really sure," Rezazadeh answered. "Certainly, he would've come across a good many goats and donkeys. Agrarian culture and all that."

"I bet Jesus was good with animals."

"He certainly had a way with fish."

Dr. Rezazadeh looked at his watch. An executive from Condé Nast was imminently due for an afternoon facial fat grafting using repurposed adipose tissue suctioned from her hindquarters.

He held a glossy tri-fold out to Lupita, filled with pictographs, histograms, and clinically unerotic photographs of body parts.

"What's this?"

"The EP brochure."

"Oh, that's alright, Rezzie. I can look it up online."

"You won't find anything online."

"No?"

He shook his head. "Not at all."

"Okay, then." Lupita frowned, taking the brochure as if she'd been handed a nose-blown handkerchief.

"Take your time looking through it. But bear in mind, it's an exploding offer. If you pass this one time, you'll never be eligible again."

"Oh." The brochure seemed weightier once she'd been told that. "I see."

Dr. Rezazadeh detected uncertainty. Cosmetic surgeons

who count themselves businessmen before physicians have a sense about these things. "You'll have the best ass in the entire city."

Lupita smiled. That was exactly what she wanted to hear.

———

A MONTH LATER, LUPITA WAS IN AN UBER HEADED TO DR. Rezazadeh's surgical suite. Candy Crush kept freezing and then quitting on her iPhone. And all her notifications were in Korean.

After her phone got all glitchy late last night, she'd hoped the problem would resolve itself.

An elusive thought manifested in an unscratchable itch on her brain. What was it she was trying to remember?

Lupita pulled the crumpled surgery instructions from her purse and read through them again. Yes, there it was, right at the bottom of the page:

"Please make sure your smartphone and EP App™ are both operable and fully updated."

Oh well.

———

LUPITA WAS HOME RECOVERING FROM HER SURGERY. HER friend Blanca had stocked her refrigerator and committed to being her temporary nurse. "I just have to run home and feed my sun conure, Buddy," Blanca qualified once Lupita was too comfortably recuperating to object, "and when I get back, I'll take care of everything." Lupita had a suspicion that Blanca's purported "bird" was a figurative reference to a booty call. It was past midnight now.

But such tawdry concerns were soon swallowed into the opiated haze facilitated by Rezazadeh's prescription pad.

The dope also touched off a sudden sugar jones.

She carefully eased out of the avocado-shaped pool float cushioning her tender posterior while she laid in bed. She shuffled like a mummy toward the fridge to inspect how Blanca had her provisioned, snugly compressed in her post-surgery garments.

Oxycodone scattered her neurons into cosmic dust.

Lupita opened the freezer bottom and feebly rummaged about.

Much to her delight, she found a pint of Häagen Dazs chocolate ice cream bookended between two boxes of year-old microwavable meals. "Blanca, you beautiful bitch." Lupita nicked a spoon from the kitchen drawer and, Häagen Dazs in hand, hobbled back to bed to watch *Love Island*.

She dry-swallowed a few more pain pills before agonizingly lowering herself into the floatie. Then, with the TV's volume turning up and spoonfuls of Häagen Dazs going down, Lupita reached an equilibrium of deep satisfaction, intoxicatedly toying with the idea of doing this for an entire two weeks.

Lupita ate the whole pint, barely able to move by the time she scraped the bottom. And in short order she sunk into dreamless sleep.

———

HOURS LATER, LUPITA ROUSED INTO TOTAL DARK'S nothingness. Her room's blackout shades were drawn, door sealed shut, television off. She pawed around for her phone, but couldn't find it. Probably wedged between the inflatable float and her mattress, she thought, or dropped by the bed frame somewhere out of her reach.

She couldn't remember the last time she'd woken up in the middle of the night and not seen the TV's multicolor blitz still burning. Lupita had never set the sleep timer on the tube in her whole life. She certainly didn't remember setting it tonight before she'd passed out.

Her room was dense with an air of chemical synthesis—like just-vulcanized rubber coming to cool, the depurated smell of burnt ozone following a storm—overpowering the jasmine and white tea from her scent diffuser. Her home's Ritz-Carltonian signature scent had decidedly soured. A stench of meat and bodily fluid joined the room's rubbery electric fragrancy, redolent of her many prior bouts of post-surgical recovery, though mildly putrid and stronger than ever before; the turned-broccoli fetor of fat necrosis, unswapped compression garments' soiled-gym-bag stink, the copper reek of bled-through bandages and dressings.

Her fingers fumbled about the unbroken dark, blindly walking the bedsheets in search of her phone. Lupita was dumbfounded at the staggering effort needed to move her arm, a physical weakness for which her recovery alone could not account. Her muscles had the syrupy lag of a body still rebooting from propofol sedation. She shivered through a febrile chill, osteoporotic pain racking her body's whole bony framework.

Lupita finally unearthed her phone, the locked screen showing near three in the morning. An EP App notification badge popped up at the bottom of the screen. She unlocked the phone to an alert flashing: "Current Caedes Asinorum Fugue™ operationality irregular. Duplicative purge initiated. Please call technical support immediately." God, she was in a fog. If she could just—

A harsh whisper cut across her bedroom's dark and silence. Lupita sucked her breath in, snuffing her phone's light against her breast. "Blanca?"

No answer. Jesus Christ, then who was there? Who could it be? Was it building maintenance here for an emergency fix? Nobody else had a key to her place. But then, why wouldn't they call out her name and turn on the lights? No. No, this wasn't that.

Oh my God. A home invasion. An intruder, here, now, breathing the same air as Lupita, occupying her same sanctuary inside her bedroom's four walls. That's why the TV was switched off.

The sharp whispering picked up, now two voices instead of one. And, a dripping sound. At first, a few trickling droplets. But it built into the drone and abrupt stops of an enlarged prostate's impinged urinary stream.

Lupita peeled the phone from her chest, but still cradled it close enough to mute its glowing diodes. Even muted, though, the screen was a tiny pole star in her room's shuttered black pitch.

Before she even dialed 911, her flight response was already telegraphing psychic maydays to a universe of nameless powers possibly willing to save her.

"911, what is the exact address of your emergency?"

Lupita's words had only just formed on her tongue when the bedroom lights switched back on. What she saw shocked her out of giving the dispatcher an answer.

There were two other Lupitas standing with their backs against her closed bedroom door. Changelings, plucked from different points on her life's timeline. And one of them was holding a baby.

To judge by the copycat's bulbous nose, the larger changeling was the pre-rhinoplasty Lupita of her freshman year of high school. The smaller one (who was holding the baby) was Lupita's ten-year-old avatar, that chubby little fourth-grade girl who was only just learning of the discomfort and self-loathing expected of little women-soon-to-be.

The baby could've been anyone's, if it was in fact a human baby. Charting its genetic heritage, however, would've been like eating soup with a fork; the infant had no nose, no nostrils, no eyes or brows or ears. There was only an inhuman mouth, full of tiered rows of spiculated lamprey teeth, rounding out a suckering circle-shaped trap.

The bodies of the two changelings (and the faceless baby) were papery wisps; the three of them could've been carried off on a stiff breeze.

"Hello? I need your location. Please give me your address," the 911 dispatcher pleaded. Lupita could hear the woman's voice, but the words were presently beyond comprehension.

The illumination of her bedroom's high hat lights exposed Lupita's body's radical transformation. Her skin's apparent translucency revealed her muscle fibers deteriorated to almost one-third their normal mass, depigmented breasts like two vacuum-sealed see-through bags with implants sewn inside them.

The fourth-grader came over to the bedside and set the baby down by the floatie, sending Lupita scurrying from her inflatable and flying across the bed, dropping her phone on the way. The fourth-grader took the cell phone and hung up the call before tossing it aside. The eyeless infant made the sound of a dozen emphysemic geriatrics simultaneously catching their breath through coughing fits. Lupita rolled off of and hid behind the far side of her king-size four-poster. The baby then laughed in the low pitch of a very big man.

"Who are you?" Lupita vocal cords were strained as if she'd spent a whole week shouting, oxygen leaking too quickly from her lungs; all that exertion, just to ask a single quiet question. A faintly reddened, yellow, serosanguinous fluid (like the ichor of healing wounds) dripped from her visitors' bodies like sweat. Damp spots appeared in the carpet under their feet. The still-chortling baby remained somehow dry.

The freshman spoke: "I are being pretty. I are maked lips. I are maked kissy lips. Breasts are become biggerer. Nice butters, big lips. Butters are being biggerer. Shape, shape—"

"Sometimes one or two of us don't come out fully cooked," the fourth-grader said, cocking her chin at the freshman. "Not that there was a surplus to work with. Who knew you'd put out three of us all at once?" The fourth-grader eyed the elder changeling while shaking her head and clucking her tongue. "There's nothing as embarrassing as seeing someone with whom you share an almost exact cellular structure turn out an imbecile." She smiled at Lupita, revealing many missing teeth, gums bloody and blackened with scurvy. She pointed at the ground and commanded the freshman: "You. Sit."

The teenage changeling folded herself cross-legged on the floor. The baby's mannish laughter devolved to deeply upsetting sucking sounds; maybe choking, maybe hungrily squalling. Its underdeveloped anatomy made that impossible to tell.

As she spoke, the elementary-age changeling pulled the freshman's head back by fingers placed under her chin. "First, let me say, there's absolutely nothing you did to cause triplication. You know, people have thoroughly forgotten the thrill of our malignant parasitism—long enough out of vogue that most can hardly credit its existence—and because of that, it bears repeating, what we do is much less science than art. What I'm saying is, don't blame yourself for the numpty's unfinished brain." She spoke in the soothing tone of a long-practicing pediatrician. "What we sometimes have to do," the fourth-grader continued, bringing her knees to press anteriorly against the freshman's scapulae, looking down to meet her eye-to-eye, their chins pointed in opposite directions, "is a consolidation."

The faceless baby crawled nearer the two changelings, seating itself with its lower legs draped over the side of the mattress. It reminded Lupita of a fisherman hanging his bare feet off the edge of a pier.

"Consolidation?" Lupita found it difficult to think.

The fourth-grader nodded. "Yes, a consolidation."

Lupita watched the would-be consolidator bend her face down toward the freshman's, the fourth-grader's mouth moving over her elder's left eye. Then, her wide-opening jaw revealed many uneven teeth, straightening themselves out, elongating on their own, while once-toothless pockets protracted new, inch-long canines.

That grotesque denticulation was not what started Lupita screaming. No, what started her screaming was what she saw those teeth doing next:

The younger one was eating the freshman's eyes.

The infant laughed and slapped its knee the way that fisherman would've at a real humdinger. Even the freshman yukked through her pain, as the younger changeling ate the jelly, and the choroids, and the extraocular muscles from her eye sockets.

By the time the pre-pubescent duplicant had finished with her meal, the infant, by virtue of some cannibalistic, co-digestive transmutation, had grown two eyes of its own.

BLANCA RETURNED TO THE APARTMENT SOMETIME AFTER sunrise. Placing her keys on the kitchen island, she called out: "Hey booty queen, I'm back! How you feeling?"

Lupita didn't answer.

Well, she must've been sleeping. Blanca would just pop her head in, see if her girl needed fresh ice or her bandages changed, a drink or a snack, whatever else.

When Blanca looked in on her friend, however, Lupita was not there. But there was a huge, plump baby, mouth greased with gore, sitting upright on the pool float atop Lupita's bed. Three skeletons stripped to no more than gristle and bone, each smaller than the other, were laid out on the floor. The baby, who despite its infancy bore all Lupita's same distinguishing features on its face, stared at Blanca in such a way to make her think she ought to close the door.

And once she'd finished screaming, that's exactly what she did.

THE BLACK GAUCHO OF REVENDICATION

None of the merchants or shopkeepers in Revendication knew where the Black Gaucho came from. Not in any exact sense. Or, if they knew, it was less in the way of nativity-as-such and more that of half-grasped myth.

The colony was an anthropoid enclave, but only the Black Gaucho was a real and red-blooded human man. Or so it went in the colonists' rumor mill colloquies.

He was the only one with five fingers per hand and thirty-two teeth (even if half were rotting out of his mouth). He chewed the *vomir* roots. Was the first, in fact, to gnaw those uncropped bitters fungating the quartzite slopes around his encampment.

He lived far, far, far outside the colony.

Was the first to snatch at their roots. He said they'd pass for tobacco in a pinch, whatever the hell that was. But it'd unzip you, too, he said, chewing the roots like that. Beware, he said, for a person's good caution would proscribe such befogging fruit.

Milt Intoh had been there when the Gaucho first found it. Or Milt did so boast to any ear that'd bend.

When the Gaucho tugged it out of the ground, no one else had ever touched it. You'd sooner drink your own piss, was how most people thought. The *vomir* evolved barbs the way helpless prey evolved spikes and spines. Needles weren't for naught. Let it prick you and it'd be hours before the blood finished flowing.

The stuff stunk all seven shades of shit. But if you chewed it or smoked it you became a living moon, and your pale light shone all over your world of night.

Five would get you ten whether that was good or bad.

With the crop's appeal becoming so known, the merchants fattened their once-razor-thin margins, wrung those last juicy ounces of profit from where once there'd been no wringing from. They weren't the first to exploit the idle mutterings of some dusty ascetic. Every godless temple had its moneychangers. Even the most distant encampment could be Greed's Tabernacle.

Outside the rhizosphere's ciphers, the Gaucho had his secrets otherwise. Occult speculations as a pastime, pitching old-world guesses at new-world problems, theoretical esoterica.

The young boys strode his flank as he followed the path to his weekly barter, cutting deals with the raggediest outfitters and swindlers, exclusively bottom-shelf. Amidst these perambulations, one of the Gaucho's adolescent devotees eavesdropped a conversation between his father and a cockeyed tweaker in his father's shop:

"Whatcher talkin' bout is an *alchemist*," the boy heard the tweaker say.

An alchemist.

Heard from one of their own and passed down the line, the boys got to playing telegraph, murmuring "alchemist" over and again until they'd reshaped the word, feeling its sound's sensation on their lips, working it between their teeth and tongues.

Fearful folk warned that the things the Black Gaucho knew were dangerous things to know, though they could but theorize on the substance of that dangerous knowledge. For their part, the merchants were happy to make their mint, attending the Gaucho pawing at the ground, watching what else he'd do, hoping they'd learn to do it themselves, and transmute that doing into saleable goods.

Of course nothing unnerves the merchant class like some misty anchorite (and the Gaucho sure as shit did). But their anxieties were flooded over by their greed.

Revendication, after all, was a place where money could be made. The only outpost in its tiny corner of space where you could walk out in the open, fresh air to breathe. A breezy oasis, in its way, appealing to men who spent their spirits with a chaser. Lost souls; rolling stones.

Through a lifetime stumbling in and out of cryostasis hangovers, through each commercial port dull as the next, without even a one-legged, two-toothed trull to bed; that's the way men came to breathe Revendication's honey-sweet open air.

Restless sailors, too, watched the Black Gaucho. The older ones, gray bearded reprobates sleeping their lives away in cargo holds, said they'd known his like, long before. They'd seen such men (they claimed), before humanity's Terminal Age brought its final atomic desolation.

Witnesses were spellbound by even his smallest cere-mony, the queerness of his ancient rites. They watched him bathe in the river, put his forehead to the dirt, gaunt and hollow from days gone without food. Their witness funded the chewing of their cud.

Some doubted there had ever even been a True Earth. And maybe there'd always be such scoffers, who laughed meanly and conspiratorially at five-fingered prophets' woo-

woo and hoodoo. "What a joke," they could say; "shit for cave-dwellers," moreover.

He said he spoke the Word. They said he'd polluted his brain.

The Word.

Yes, they laughed, they mocked the Word. But the truth? They lived in fear of its unaccountable power. Because the children, anywhere children might be found, heard the mystic call.

They didn't care if the Word was real. The children knew if you believed in it, then anything could be as real as it needed to be. They hungered, for legend, for superstition. "Truth" was an irrelevancy.

Since knee-high, colonists would come as soon as they could crawl and sit at the Black Gaucho's feet. They would listen to him. Listen to him speak the Word and, in so doing, change themselves. They felt like they'd become the glowy shine of the three moons in the sky.

An alchemist.

Tell us the Word again, please, they'd ask him. And tell us what it means, they'd say.

And the Black Gaucho would nod, eyes shadowed under his wide-brimmed hat, bushy chin dribbly spackled, having always only just chewn the root. He would nod and say, "I can tell you the Word," he'd say. "But I can't tell you what it means no more."

And the merchants' striplings said they'd take that, too.

He would take off his wide-brimmed hat, bend his leg and set it down. And the shavers and nippers would follow his flailing arms, goggle-eyed, see him sleying his yarns through an invisible loom, drawing skeins from and of the past, never once launching the hat from his knee. And he'd give them the Word:

"'For the word of God is living and active, sharper than any two-edged sword, piercing to the division of soul and spirit, of joints and marrow, and discerning the thoughts and intentions of the heart.' That is the very Word Itself, children." Sometimes he'd spit a bit more, sometimes a little less, but once he'd spent his tongue, the Gaucho closed his ministry the same way: "Now each of you got your share. So go on out and live it."

"But what does it mean?" Samit never failed to ask. Samit, colony-born runt of the litter; Samit, who wanted to know more than anyone else, though he didn't know what. But there was something, something in the Word, something to get himself unshackled, set free, seeing back to places of fallen myth, seeing sights he'd never seen. "What does it mean?"

"It don't mean nothing no more," was the only answer the Gaucho ever gave.

Everything that lived or breathed in Revendication watched him—the kids with their glittering eyes, the consternated nailbiters, the stoop-sweeping mamalois angry at his dead letters and terrified of his mysticalizing tongue— even the goldbricking hustlers—they would all watch the Black Gaucho, and they would all wonder, to a man, woman and child, about all his weird words and lore. About Earth. About the Word.

Inevitably, one of the colony elders closed out their sessions of shit-shooting with the final say:

"There was once a world full of such men. But I believe him to be the last."

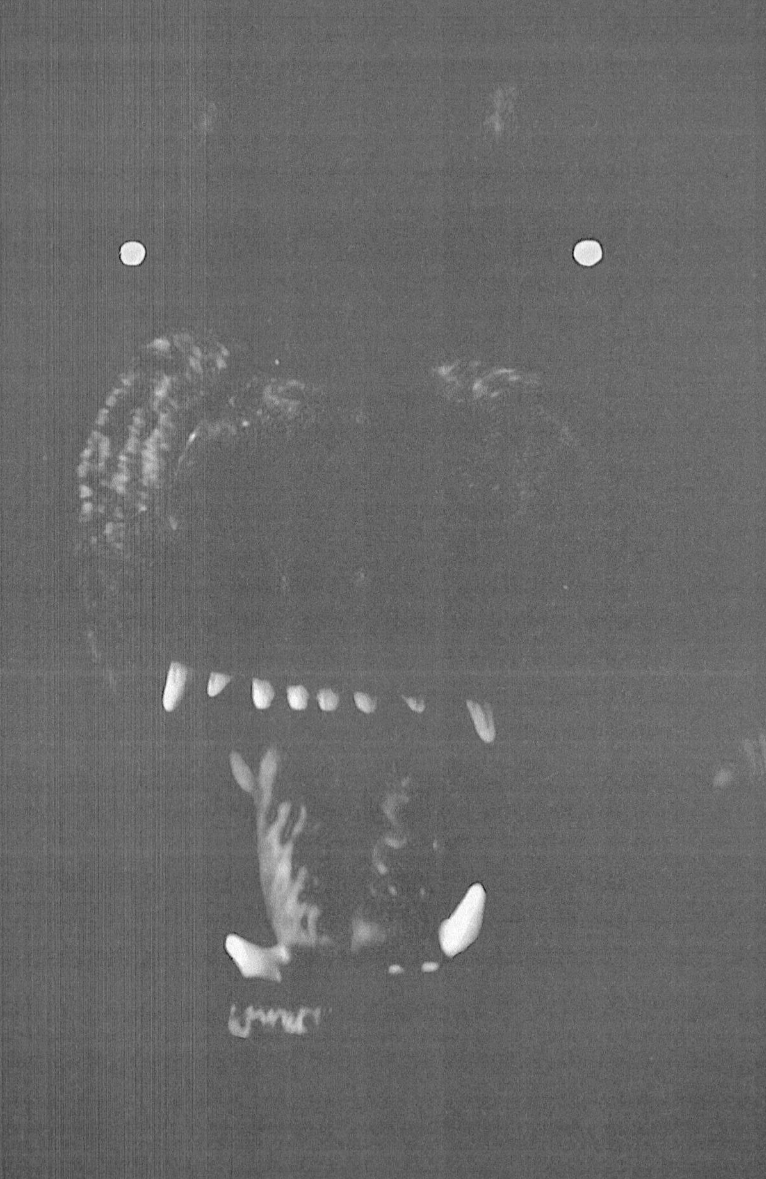

THE GOLDEN MILE

(A NOTE TO THE READER: ORIGINALLY PUBLISHED IN MACABRE MAGAZINE. APPEARS BY SPECIAL PERMISSION OF MACABRE MAGAZINE EDITOR JIMMY BLAKEMORE.)

I see the new associate curator for Costume and Textiles waving me over. It's the end of the day and it would be smarter to pretend that I don't see her. But what sane man ignores a pretty woman waving at him? So I go.

Am I surprised when Bethany asks me, "Dave, can you help me move something?"

No, I am not surprised.

But I'm already out of my uniform. And for the last three hours all I've been thinking about is getting a hoagie from Wawa in time to dodge the rain home.

Bethany is very attractive, but that's rather a moot point with her being so astronomically far out of my league. So I'm inclined to beg off. Single, unmarried men tend to be selfish that way.

"Lonnie is…" She hesitates. Higher education disposes her to a too-judicious phrasing of her grievance. "He's in a mood."

Lonnie, the mercurial Collections Storage manager, has been repositorist of every exhibitable item in the museum over the last thirty-four years. He's a bit of a tin-pot dictator. And like many other gatekeepers of such durable tenure, thinking themselves untouchable (and so dispensing with social niceties), Lonnie's long since turned meaner than a snake.

Human beings should visit Lonnie with no more frequency than they attend funerals.

Well, I suppose a little esprit de corps won't hurt me.

"Okay, what're we getting?"

"Nothing spectacular," she says. "A bequest from some memorabiliaist with a hard-on for the circus."

I raise my eyebrows. "You can explain on the way."

THERE ARE NO WINDOWS DOWN IN COLLECTIONS STORAGE and the artificial light is dim. A swirling musk of vinegary decomposing plastics, vanilla-and-almond-scented drifts of centuries-old paper, and varnish lingering since the Industrial Revolution combine with innumerable other notes of fine art's decay to create the archival smell.

Lonnie is surely wandering amongst the stacks. A half-open steamer trunk with the drawbolts unlatched sits in front of the industrial desk from which he spits invective at the art couriers and preparators. The trunk is blocking a sign on which is written: "EATING IN STORAGE = FIRED." No idle warning. On top of his desk is the anachronism of a handwritten logbook, and on the latest entry page:

"Description: various circus costumes, sundry; Estate of Armandina Mehrman-Geigenbecken. Requested by: Bethany Lê. Authorized by: Leonard Schwerner."

Lonnie's signed her out already and time-stamped the release authorization with his rotary stamp (which also belongs in a museum). I crouch and grab one end of the trunk.

"This is it, right? A bunch of circus stuff?"

"Yeah, but…" Bethany warily regards the no man's land of pull-out racks, hanging systems, sealed cabinets and cradles. She reverts to me with a look I've seen on the faces of people who don't know which is the right SEPTA train home. I stand back up.

"It'll be fine," I say. "Just sign your name in the logbook. He's already filled it all out."

She looks back and forth between me and the stacks. "You think?"

"Listen, you can just tell him I came and got it myself. Lonnie won't yell at me, he likes me."

"Is that true?"

"Absolutely," I say, lying through my teeth. Lonnie has in fact called me "as useful as a single chopstick" and said that he'd "prefer a root canal on a hot tooth with no lido- caine" to my company.

Bethany smiles and says, "Alright, let's do it," before crouching down to grab her side.

She grips the handle. And immediately wrenches her hand back with a bloodcurdling scream.

I startle. "What happened?" I say.

Bethany holds her hand up, blood visibly gushing from her palm. She runs out into the basement hall. I think she might be crying. It certainly sounds like she's crying.

I am somewhat in shock and do not yet move.

There is a surprising amount of blood on the top of the trunk. A banded tongue of gold-studded leather sticks out the side. Blood flows downslope of the trunk's tilted closure and spills onto the band. And then something happens. The air is charged with foreboding, a palpable surge of cosmic radiation. I am (magnetically) drawn to the studded (now-bloodied) band; a ten-thousand-ton impulse moves me to take it. I work it out of its wedge.

It's a well-worn dog collar, too big for any dog I've ever seen. Old but high quality and clean, a leatherworker's special order. The leather is spangled gold with studs and spikes, a tarnished brass plate mounted halfway along the length of the collar, on which is written: "KLEON, EIGENTUM VON KLAUS GEIGENBECKEN". Below that, the inscription: "*Ein Clown, ein Hund, ein Teufel. Das Geschöpf meines Herzens.*"

I can't explain why I do what I do next. It certainly would've been caught by the security camera's sweeping lens. Nevertheless, I take a dust cloth from Lonnie's desk and wrap the dog collar inside of it. I stuff the cloth-wrapped collar in my cargo shorts' side pocket, and thereon depart, to Bethany if I can, to find her and her injury out.

———

It takes all of three minutes to get my hoagie. I still don't beat the rain.

At home, I fall asleep on my couch holding the dog collar, leather band still tacky with Bethany's blood. A nightmare, mystifying and vivid, visits me in my sleep:

———

Legging it toward Arch Street, there's a city block paved with granite cobblestone. That street is now surfaced with the soles of dress shoes facing bottoms-up. All different sizes, and all very long, they share in common the irregularity that where the sole anchors the toe box is wider than the whole rest of the shoe.

"You must be the thief."

I turn to find my apparent addressor standing in front of the Comcast Technology Center. A bag lady, wearing the national uniform of trampdom—self-sheared fingerless gloves, a blotched and holey hooded sweatshirt, longline coat the same color as soot—is eyeballing me with clinical directness. Even through her unseasonable layering, I discern a bust size only otherwise seen on diabetic city bus drivers and in reality TV tales of redemptive weight loss.

Most notable, however, is her face.

It is not the facial hair of a slight congenital hirsutism, but the beard of a veteran of the Civil War. Or an Old Testament prophet. A bearded lady. I'm looking at a bearded bag lady.

"What'd you say?"

"You must be the thief," she repeats, staring, coldly staring. "Because here I am, your very Cassandra. And by the by, my harbingering has never harbingered the wrong harbingee. Think of me as your executive soothsayer. There's nobody else, on earth, for me, right now, but you."

Instead of mirroring the sun, the Center's towering façade of glass and steel reflects back vertical red and white stripes running the height of the building.

"He won't be long in his arrival. I'm sure he's bringing the others, too."

"Who?" I turn and look behind me for the stripes seen in the tower's glass reflection, but find only a Presbyterian church. I turn back towards her.

"Ever heard of 'The Great Geigenbecken Circus'?"

I shake my head. "No."

She conjures a cigarette from the ether, igniting it with a lighter concealed behind her thumb, or possibly by her thumb itself. "Geigenbecken was a true animal lover. A bit ahead of his time in that way. Big on reward when all other trainers still punished. Worked the pachyderms and ponies, the jungle cats—the big ticket beasts, you know." She takes a pull on her cigarette and vents a smoky-low cackle. "Used to kiss the tuskers, dance with the monkeys. Pleasant enough fellow. A pleasure to work for."

Her hoarse voice is a soporific; it drags me into stupor. I don't know why I'm listening, but I'm unable to stop.

I hear the steam-powered whistle of a calliope in the distance.

Walking my way, the bag lady smiles teeth like kernels of blue corn through neon-indigo smoke. I expect a wave of gin, old urine, and stale cigarettes to accompany her, but I smell nothing. Less than nothing, in fact; a vacuum, the hungry suck of an abyss. What should be the whites of her eyes are concrete-gray, the irises charcoal-black.

"Klaus Geigenbecken. Haven't heard of him either?"

"No."

"Kleon the Talking Clown Dog?"

"Who?"

She exhales a luminescent vapor no human has ever exhaled. "I'll take that as a 'no'. Kleon was Klaus Geigenbecken's dog. That's whose collar you took."

I lie. "I didn't take anything." I am possessive of the collar, solicitous of its safe keeping. "I don't know about any collar." My avarice is someone else's. Why should I be acquisitive over something I don't own? But I am.

"Listen to me," she says. "Listen to me close. This is not something to be trifled with. Geigenbecken's molossus is possessed of inexhaustible hunger. Lain dormant, yes, for a time. But your blood on the collar will have whetted its appetite."

"It wasn't my blood."

She smiles. It's not a happy one. "So you do know about the collar."

I look around the empty street. I smell a refinery and a zoo. There is no one anywhere at all. I hear no engines, no footsteps, no bustle, no shouting or honking horns. A powder-keg-tension pervades the atmosphere, air thickened to riots' precipitating dew point. Small mercies: there's no rioters to be found.

She rushes me without running, as if a ratty overcoat shunted along the slick rail of a dry cleaner's conveyor. Her eyes come close enough to crawl into my own. She has no scent, gives off no heat. But she emits a pulse of nauseating energy. I feel the sensation, I imagine, of being implanted with a pacemaker then dropped in the eye of a geomagnetic storm. She bares her teeth at me, jaw gaped exaggeratedly wide so I ought to see down her throat; but there is nothing past her teeth—no tongue, no mucosa, no uvula, no blood-flowing flesh—nothing except lightless emptiness of limitless depth.

Her voice is lupine and low and berserker-wild, words growling out her gut in a mangle. But her cadence is nothing against the terror of the consumptive void inside of her throat. I do not move a whit, scared shitless I'll somehow fall into her gorge.

"Klaus bought that dog without currency to purchase. Do you know what happens when you contract gold and blood for consideration, but only bring the gold?"

I shake my head.

"The aggrieved party remedies the breach." She touches my face and I vomit inside my closed mouth. But the ejecta's an illusion, and my mouth isn't closed.

"Geigenbecken's dog isn't one as such," she says, her fingertips tracing lines of anathema over my skin. "It is most literally a hellhound. The genuine article, reared by the ferryman himself. Reared on damnation's very river. Weaned on the gold pieces that tolled the dead's river crossing; who'd tested the coins against its teeth and tasted the toll on its tongue. A whelp grown to a molossus, accompanying the sculler shuttling the dead to Tartarus. In Tartarus, boy, where conspiracy took shape. A conspiracy of blood, to feed the souls of the dead and enflesh them with bodies. A conspiracy of gold to fund limitless passage over the river of the dead. An army of revenants roving past their river boundary to raid the living world—what does that amount to?"

Nothing good, I think, but hold my tongue.

"Hell on earth. So to speak. Geigenbecken's dog is a hellhound traded for a promise of lifeblood and gold. That's who you're inviting to your table. I'd get the lead out, boy. Wash your blood from his collar."

"It wasn't my blood," I'm sure I think and don't say. At any rate, she hears me.

"Whoever's blood. Wash it clean. Maybe there's still time. Maybe the signal's not yet got…" She seems to think for a moment. "Amplitude."

She turns into a portal supported with planks and a frame of weathered, dry-dirtied wood. It's like an entrance into an old mine from the time of the gold rush. She stops at its threshold, before the baptismal font of unending darkness. I am convinced the abyss is in her throat, that the portal leads there, that she is bound for the depthless emptiness inside her own person. She looks back to me and says, "You'll know it when you see it. The dog dressed as a clown."

A hair's breadth from her immersion, I call out after: "Why a clown?"

Her voice is liquid, reverberant; she's seeping into the portal's pitch: "I find that fiends operate on the basis of acquisition and destruction. If they invert their perverse buffoonery to horror, that's just a variation on a theme. What accounts for ghouls' humor, I really can't say…"

———

I WAKE UP STILL HOLDING THE DOG COLLAR. My undershirt is drenched in animal-smelling sweat. Stripes of sunlight bleed through my blinds to stir nausea in my belly. There is acid in my brain.

More than a dozen text messages from Bethany wait on my phone to be read. The first text was sent right after I left work; I'd looked at my phone since then, I should've noticed it.

My phone was with me the whole night; I should've noticed all of them.

First, Bethany relays that she's at the emergency room. A few texts later, that her doctor's diagnosis was septicemia. The succeeding messages descend into a bizarre garble of medical updates on the risk of septic shock and intercessory pleas better directed toward a being of less negligible omnipotence than my own (that is to say, who has more power than none). The last message reads: "I'm going to die now, David."

Nothing after that.

I'm mainlining a hot dose of panic. There is a culpability I bear, I'm certain. Counteractive measures must be taken. I move quickly and without thought.

I walk the seven blocks west to the riverside park, holding the gold-spiked collar, and follow the path out to the bicyclists' causeway raised over the river. I stand at the railing. The color of the Schuylkill River is the color of split pea soup. Its placidity is misleading in light of its history; floods that can wash train cars from their tracks, a thousand cesspits of dumped sewage swirling in its currents.

I throw the collar into the river, childishly hoping it will be carried off to sea.

I go home to clean myself and rehearse an alibi whose necessity is superfluous.

I have a guilty mind. Guilt is another thing altogether.

———

Museum Mile undergoes a transfiguration of its boulevard of many nations' flags. These changes, in their beginnings, seem only slight.

Albania's two-headed eagle spreads black wings of dominion over its bell-pepper-red field, flag rippling in the wind, changing, until the bold red leaches to the smutty mustard-yellow of sweat-stained sheets. Soon there is no black eagle, surrendered to the likeness of a dog. A Mastiff-dwarfing devourer from a bloodier long-ago.

Dressed like a clown.

Its gravestone-gray fur is smeared greasepaint-white around the muzzle, abrasions glistening cherry-red on its skinned snout, gory rhinarium replacing the ball of red foam. No bowling-pin-shaped derby shoes but skulls shaved into boots. No gaudy sunflower boutonnière with a sucker-spritzing squeeze bulb, but a shriveled paw amputated from some unknown species, pinned into the brisket of the clown-dog's chest.

It might be taken for a gormless riff on Coolidge's dogs playing poker. But this is not that. The flag's depiction is of an animal calculating in its menace. Less a four-legged Bozo than a canid Joseph Stalin quietly contemplating the liquidation of kulaks while in his Kremlin study.

An epigraph bleeds itself into the flag, materializing Gothic characters with harsh ligatures, evoking corrupted grimoires' incantations; except, the message is so very mundane: "KLEON IS GOLD. BUY GOLD FOR YOU. BUT GIVE GOLD FOR KLEON."

I stroll beneath the Mile's many banners, and around me grows a stranger day. The London plane trees coloring the Parkway green and lush grow corroded mantles that look like rusted barbed wire hung from weeping willows. All the crispness of spring yields to a miasma bringing to mind a river overflowing with spoiled pigs' blood.

I hear the screeching ululations of mentally-ill women at a bazaar. Turning back to Logan Square, I see two nuns shoving an old man to the ground right next to the fountain. One of the sisters rips the man's cane from his brittle hands and begins to beat him with it. They smile when they see me watching them. Every drooling tooth in both their heads has a gold crown.

The background of every successive country's flag along my walk progresses to perspirant-yellow, then nearer the shitty barbotine-brown of fungated potatoes. Kleon flutters from all of them with a stone-cold killer's unwavering gaze.

The messages grow more pointed:

"KLEON IS NECESSARY. BUY GOLD AND GIVE IT TO HIM. HE WILL PROTECT YOUR GOLD FROM THOSE PLANNING TO SLAUGHTER YOUR LOVED ONES WITH KNIVES."

And:

"THOSE WITHOUT GOLD WILL SUFFER. THOSE WHO DO NOT OBTAIN AND REMIT GOLD TO KLEON WILL SUFFER."

I stop walking, and search for other apparent witnesses to this utter madhouse shit.

A man watches me from under the pediment of the Rodin Museum's porticoed entrance, sipping iced coffee through a straw. I wave at him. He chucks the iced coffee at me but misses, then bolts like I'm his bookie.

A municipal work crew set up on the treescaped promenade between opposing traffic flows is swapping out a Finnish flag for another depicting Kleon. They're using a telescopic bucket truck like the ones PECO Energy uses. One man removes the Finnish flag while another sets traffic cones around the truck. A third man stands in idle witness.

This third man is exceptionally large. To look at him, City Hall could substantially trim their landscaping budget letting him uproot all of Philadelphia's dead trees by himself (and further write off the cost of wood waste disposal by letting him eat them, too).

"Hey!" I yell. "Hey man, what the hell's going on here?"

I break into a trot toward the crew. The crane operator looks at me with the indifference given inanimate objects; I might as well be a mailbox. But the man placing the parking cones makes eye contact. His eyes remind me of the look on my middle-school buddy Chris Weir's face when his dipso old man turned up after sleepovers to remand Chris to the Weirs' domestic hellhole.

I choose to approach the overmuscled third, a decision based, quite possibly, on nothing more than the vague cinematic logic of prison movies.

"What the hell are you guys doing?"

"Um. Hanging stuff," the behemoth says.

"What's with the flags? People are going to be pissed off." Philadelphians appreciate radical change as much as they enjoy eating cheesesteak with a fork.

The man rubs his fingers into pretzels and knots. "I—um—we're doing flags. I thought flags was okay to hang."

His toothy smile broadcasts nervous tension. A short-bread-sweet grin—overly sweet, in fact, for a mug that ugly. I size him up. He wears a burgundy-colored wristband with "GRYFFINDOR" debossed on the band in honey-gold. He's avoiding eye contact, fighting an impulse to check me staring.

"Ma said it was okay to dress up."

"Dress up like what?" I say. And the moment I ask, I see. Maybe I have a brain tumor that I didn't see it till now.

The heat beads greasepainted sweat on his moony face, trickling from his Neanderthalic brow down his utility-pole-thick neck. A cubic-zirconia-bedazzled dog collar wraps around his throat. Given his size, it could be a teenager's belt from Hot Topic. He looks like some effete TikToker's carrier-purse-pet mated with Bam Bam Bigelow.

His speech halts across our further exchange, and after not very long I realize his mental disability. With this come to light, I pivot closer to a bookmobile driver's wonders-of-literacy whimsy. Notwithstanding his now-diminished disquiet, I still feel like a monumental dick.

"Can I ask you somethin'?" he says.

"Sure, pal."

"You brung gold?" His question is hopeful, if not meek. With the air of a child impersonating an adult, he says, "Gold's important. They said it's good for everyone."

My instinct is to reassuringly pat him on the shoulder, but I think there are unwritten rules about these sorts of interactions and I'm not sure what they are. What I do know is that bursting his bubble is a level of assholery I'm unwilling to approach. "I'm going to go get some right now, big guy. Just wanted to come let you know that's what I was doing. Keep up the good work."

"Okay!" His enthusiasm raises his right hand's outfacing palm. I can tell he's restraining himself when we high-five, but it still hurts.

I try not to pity him. No, I don't pity him. I don't. Pity is an emotion of projected superiority. He's happy but, even if he's not, it's not my business. I take the world as it is, not as it should be. I tell myself that's what I do. I almost believe it.

"You're doing good, too," he says. He hesitates before adding, "big guy."

He blue-ribbons our interaction with a meaty thumbs-up. I give one back and feel okay about how I've handled things.

I almost forget the dog.

———

I AM A GUEST & PROTECTION SERVICES ASSOCIATE. Meaning I dissuade wayward children from rubbing their grubby fingers on oil paintings and explain the self-directed audio tour guides to senior citizens. Excitement's a rarity. Though, I once intercepted a metalhead coven bowing to Rauschenberg's stuffed goat while playing Slayer's "Angel of Death" full blast from a cell phone. Moving them along while stifling my laughter, I told them they could praise the Dark Lord elsewhere.

Otherwise it's mostly tedium.

Not today.

As I pass the West Entrance into Lenfest Hall, the smell hits me. It is a zoological funk of creatures' fibrous shits, acrid urine, straw bedding in cages, grassy feed and kibble. But it's the aroma of the midway, too; popcorn fresh from the kettle and warm salted peanuts, swirling cotton candy and leakily-tapped kegs.

Sasha Weissman, the Director of the museum, passes me going in. She is naked except for oversized red-sequined shorts held up with furry blue suspenders only just covering her nipples. She has greasepaint on her face and holds three empty leashes, all wet with blood. She is a known third-wave feminist who rode in the Philly Naked Bike Ride last year. I decide to say nothing.

Neither of the unapologetically-upbeat Cynthia or Kofi wait at the visitor services desks. At Cynthia's station is a taxidermy mount of Kleon dressed as on the flags flown over the Mile.

I examine the taxidermy more closely.

Its size is staggering, close to a mountain lion's. It has Kleon's same nose scraped wet cherry-red, grungy fur matted gunmetal-gray, and the paraphernalia of a violently perverted clownery. I don't hear or feel but sideways-sense hidden organic functions; blood flowing, cognition's electrical impulses, invisible footprints and echoes of movement. These are rumors, not sounds.

Glistening tears well up Kleon's eyes. I hear the stifled grunts of a hostage through a gag.

I am in a lair of abstruse lethality.

In this different life than mine, this exotic and inescapable tale I am now in, I am made to suffer again (and vividly) through all my old hurts. I reexperience the anguish of bad breakups with good women, the vertiginous rebounds to succubine honeytraps, the inescapability of both; I relive my parents' premature deaths and unpayable debts, the purgatory of probate court to follow; reacquaint myself with the throttling dread of learning my brother was shattered by a pickup truck riding his bike to summer school, sit out an open sentence in waiting rooms while doctors induce his medical coma and perform his many surgeries; all this, and the despondency of the long nights succeeding those many terrible days.

I am choking now, choking, and reaching for Kleon's tear-swollen eyes.

"Gold," something inaudibly whispers from where my thoughts begin. "Gold with no laws, gold to metamorphose, gold for the god whose dark year has returned. Gold blooms of incest, gilt parasite and teratoma, gold that the wretched stains be blotted. Gold in the god's dark year of return. And more than all else, blood for gold. Blood for gold…"

The voice continues as I tear through Lenfest Hall into the heart of the museum.

———

I AM HUNTED BY MEMORIES AND THE VOICE. A REVELATION will soon come, this I somehow know. An antidote soon administered. An audit that I might pay my debts. A wholesale erasure and reconstruction of my person. Judgment. Penance. Rebirth.

I catch my breath before entering to change into uniform.

Inside the locker room, sitting at the bench in front of his locker, is my work-friend Larry. I see him remove his badge and unbutton his blue Allied Security shirt. Larry cries as he changes clothes.

"What's going on?" I say. My preoccupation with the day's Grand-Guignol is overcome by the anxieties of our daily bread. "Are they firing people?"

Larry doesn't answer, now stripped down to his undershirt and boxers, his uniform left lying on the floor. He drags his backpack out from under the bench and fishes around inside it. Then pulls out a gift-wrapped box.

"What's that?"

Larry peels away the decorative paper and opens the box. I watch; I am confused. My heart beats an irregular time signature. Larry takes a clear plastic rectangular case labeled "GRAFTOBIAN" out of the unwrapped box and opens it.

He dabs his face with a cosmetic sponge dipped in greasepaint from the opened case. The greasepaint muddies his tears.

"Larry?"

Sobbing, he opens his mouth to speak. His gums are clotted with jellied bulbs of blood where his gold-capped teeth have been pulled.

"To give myself to him with gold, to give itself to him, gold for it all, to give all myself for him. He needs to come back to come back alive." Larry is whinging through his mouth's bloody sludge. "They are treasurers of beasts and beasts of blood and treasure. It's shown me and I choose it, David. And he..." Larry looks down at his chest and taps his middle finger to his sternum, a little to the left of it. "I'll carry it inside me. So blood be with gold, and gold be in the blood."

His face is terrible to see when he looks at me; altered unto permanent derangement. His smile frightens me, the smile of knowing a great secret that does not truly exist; my stomach turns at saliva unspooling bloody mess from his mouth. "There is a place, a secret place, a place we can all call home." His cadence is almost a sing-song.

"Larry..." I am repulsed by his lunacy, evolution urging psychopathological avoidance. I want Larry to die to watch his corpse chucked in a dumpster; I'll scour his malignancy from me with antiseptic soap. But, then, also, to partake in his madness. A voluptuary aching inside me, a cancer of appetitive delights; a newborn sadism, to tear flesh and break bones; inside me, a violent sensualist begging for release.

Which of any of these feelings are not my own?

"Larry, what do you mean?"

He rummages in his backpack again. Stupefaction precedes my awareness of the gun in his hand. When I realize he is armed, I slam my back into the wall of lockers behind me. "Larry…"

He presses the barrel in toward his heart. I wonder if I can bend my wrist the same way he's bending his now, if it would bend all the way in toward ending my own life.

"Gold with blood." A voice of insubstantial physical element speaks to me. "Gold with death, gold with blood, gold in blood, gold inside of death's blood…"

His gunshot bullhorns in our close quarters. It is dynamite exploded in my ear canal. My heart is molten-hot with boiling diastoles and systoles. I have the ejection fraction of a volcano.

("Gold with blood, gold for death, bloody gold for the god…")

Gunpowder smoke smells differently than I imagined—I can't remember ever firing a gun, though I'm sure I have. Everything is new in a terrible way. My body quakes as violently as it can short of tonic-clonic seizure. Larry is dead. ("Gold with blood, in death's blood, the lust of blood-lusting gold…") Larry is dead. ("Eat the treasures of hearts holding ingots, drink your death down from crucibles of blood…")

Larry is dead.

I don't want to look. But dying, and death, and the

bloody spume in death's wake, must all of them be witnessed; somehow I know this thing I've never known before. It is the vestigial instinct of speechless hominids prostrating themselves at roaring, crackling thunderheads.

Larry sputters his last breath through his lips, not red but brightly gilt; the tip of his tongue, his bottom teeth, all brushed with gold leaf. His wound hemorrhages glitter. I see pure gold casting grains spilt from the gunshot hole in Larry's chest; the perceptual boundary between worldly phenomenon and phantasmagoria is obliterated.

("Gold with blood, gold for death, bloody gold for the god…")

I cry while collecting death's treasure trove. Blood materializes on the metal lifted from Larry's fatal wound. It glistens on grains of gold.

Filling up Larry's backpack takes time. When there is no more gold to be collected, I prod Larry's wound to see what will jar loose. (The disembodied voice continues whispering of "…bloody gold for the god…") I push the wound until it erupts the evacuated contents of a golden abscess.

I wade through clouds of exploded gunpowder thickening and turning, stinking closer to coal fire and bubbling tar than spent ammunition. Particles of light scatter in the smoke.

I am like a heister grabbing cash against wailing sirens, filling up Larry's bag. A disembodied pursuer, somewhere out there, stoking me in frenzy; driven, I am driven, the slavedriver's pointillated face formed in light particles inside smoke, barking commands that cannot be ignored.

("Gold with blood, gold for death, bloody gold for the god…")

I lever the weight too quickly swinging the backpack to

my shoulder, tipping myself over, a runaway anchor. Somehow, I do not fall.

I explode through the locker room's double doors, fly through the vestibule, hurtle up the stairs at the side wall. My debts and misdeeds chase behind me, a platoon of roaring wretches—no hands and no feet and no eyes—with slithering bellies and unendingly hungry hookworm mouths. Memory's bone-crushing weight bears down on me, and I flee toward revelation, toward unknowable consequence. The voice wants to guide me to the home we all live in before pain and fear and before life begins.

The weight of the overloaded backpack, my mad dash up the stairs—my legs and lungs revolt.

I come careening out of the stairwell on a kamikaze course toward the European Art galleries. I hardly stop myself before I almost barrel into the hirsute harpy in her longline coat. I juke, I narrowly avoid the collision, but I snag my back ankle on my front, and I fall forward. Face-first into the ground.

———

Maybe knocked out cold? My head an overheated water bladder. On my stomach, cold from the floor.

I roll my back onto lineoleum—ears ring, field of vision tremulates till it blurs—my brain, swollen inside the pressure-cooker of my battered skull. My tongue is numb, motor control at half-speed.

I see the bearded lady standing over me.

"Tried telling you," she says to me. "Told you to wash off the blood. And what do you do? You chuck it in the trough this whole toxic city drinks from…" A violent arena roars its rage outside; the museum shakes to its foundation and the walls and ceiling moan. "You don't know what you've done," she says, and the fear in her voice is more terrifying than anything. "The shades of Tartarus are here."

Gallery lights shutter in a cascade of loud low-end switches, contactors mechanically clunking as they disengage. Every window, sealed off from the sun. In the distance, at a range the museum's physical dimensions don't cover, there is a fire climbing higher than the roof would've been. I see Kleon illuminated in its broiling light; his size is galling, no matter the distance. He gnashes the bloody ribs of a dead or dying horse.

Standing near the dog is a chinbearded older man donned with Homburg hat. He wears a funereal business frock suit with a waistcoat beneath, a black bulldogger tie under his dress shirt collar.

The sound of the calliope, the roaring of lions and trumpeting of elephants, the applause and clamor of an astonished crowd. Outside, the entire city screams. Kerosene vapors slither up my nose and down my throat. The fire blazes, bright, so, so bright. And I see that I am no longer in the museum. But I am inside a circus tent, the screaming city fading into another reality, beyond the creeping dark.

But there is mercy. My memories are dead here. My memories, my debts. There is only blood and gold.

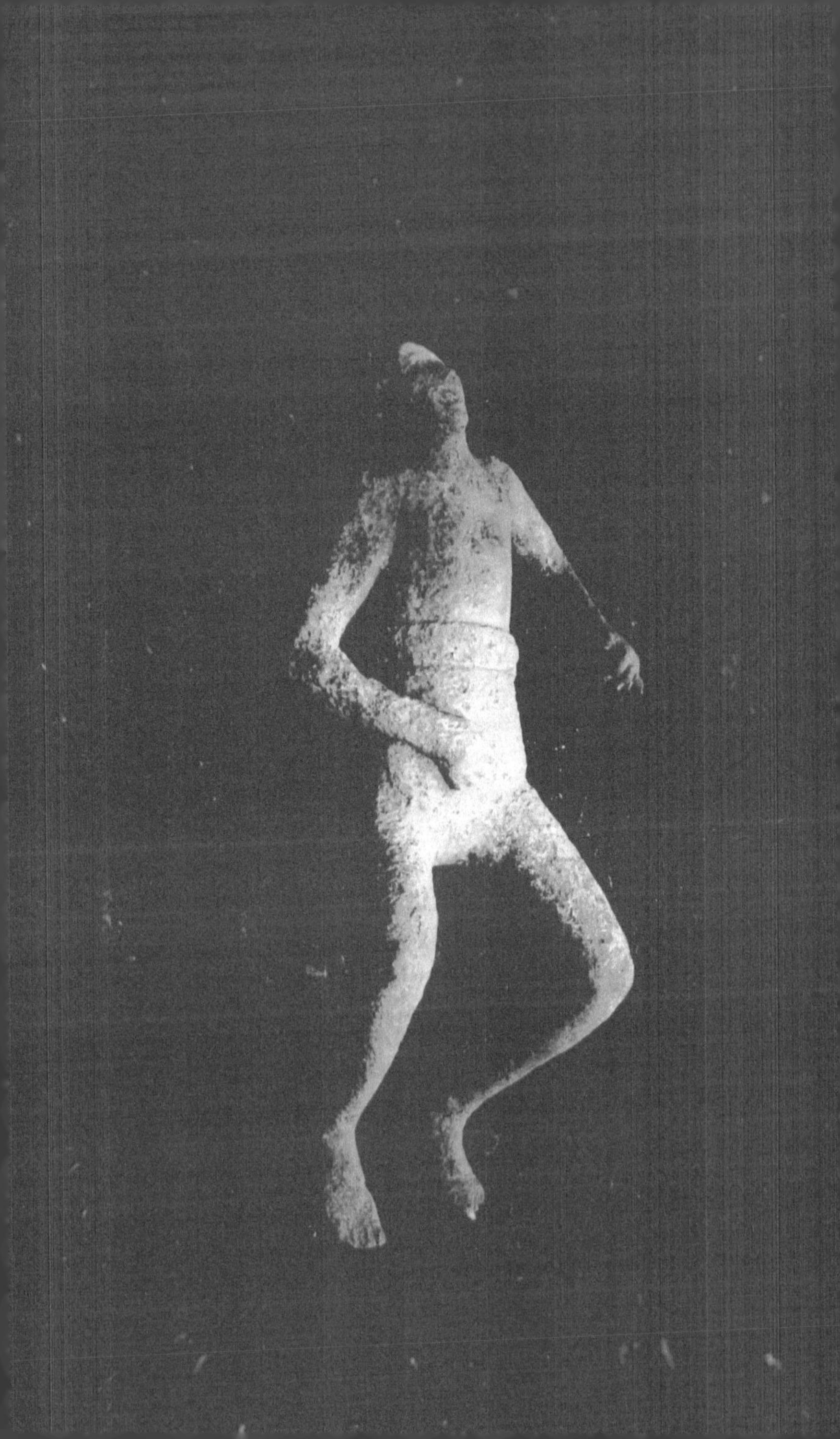

IN A NEW WORLD, ITS BASEMENT

Everything changed, all in a microscopic moment. Maybe it was when the anesthesiologist started my propofol drip. Sometime between my blood sleeping and my body waking. Somewhere in there.

I came to on a gurney behind a bedsheet curtain. The world sounded artificial, like I was sitting in a waiting room leading into the edifice that housed the whole of reality. Everything was almost the same, only three shades darker. A little more humid, a little bit wetter. Some noise was muted and delayed, lagging a step behind its originating event, volume mismatched. An almost-percussive drone underlay all sound.

Dull and distant, I heard tinnitus's unbroken ring—like electric stovetops complaining at a pan set down wrong on a burner, television static blending behind unconscious thought, battery-change warnings from smoke detectors, wire service bells singing on an eternal radio frequency, echoing, echoing on and on.

A nurse brought my discharge papers, the same as always. Promise you'll pay your bills, don't sue us if you die (or are transfused with a disease, or missing the organ you came in with), the same old boilerplate. Except, on the last page: DO YOU CONSENT TO DEBTORS' PRISON AND/OR SERVICE IN A WORK COLONY IF YOU ARE UNABLE TO PAY YOUR BILL?

There was only one answer I could choose, and it was already Xed out for me:

YES ☒

———

I LEFT THE HOSPITAL. A MAN WAS BEGGING FOR CHANGE ON the closest corner. A beggar with a very unbeggarly look, without that schizophrenic air of grizzled prophecy. Clothes moth-bitten but very, very clean.

He bumrushed me after I made accidental eye contact. "Please, help me. I need money to buy back my daughter." His callused but well-scrubbed hands fumbled at my shirt collar. He smelled like a scared animal doused in industrial detergent. "There's no deal that can't be unmade. They said that to me. They said it! I need to get her back, I need my little girl back. With all her fingers and toes. But where's the breadline? There ain't no breadline to stand in. They keep her in the Basement. But they don't feed me so I can get her, don't let me work to buy her back out. How can I get her out if I ain't got the work to buy her back out?"

"What basement?"

The bum looked confused by my question, as if I were asking what shape a square is or what color grass grows.

He spat out polysyllabic dribble before eventually locating his language. "They're—they're making all widows and orphans." He was cracked out, and his eyes were just as cracked out as him—methhead wildman eyes, I thought, their droughted red ravines of blood divvying up desiccated whites. "What good it'll do 'em then, huh?" He got close enough to hiss in my ear; I smelled mouthwash on his breath and thought maybe he'd been drinking Listerine. The paradox of a disordered mind in a hygienic vessel.

"Ain't nothin' to me but my name and the ones I named." I tried to get away but he gripped my collar tight using both his hands, pulled me in nose-to-nose. "Ain't nothin' to none of us but the ones we named! What else is left? Dammit, what else is left?"

I was about to give him a good shove, but the wet-earred wackadoo was dragged off before I could. This interdiction came at two flatfoots' behest—like squaddies done up in glossy, ink-black jackboots, better-suited to goosestepping than walking a beat. Tar-black beatcops. The two of them bagged the beggar, each grabbing one of his elbows. I watched them carry the madman off toward Shanghai.

"You can't do this to me," the beggar babbled on, "this isn't how we live—I'm still a man, ain't I? I'm not low like dogs. I'm still a man! My daughter is waiting on me, I need to see her home!"

One goonish patrolman punched the beggar in the gut, stopping his raving to put him down on his knees. Violence visited an epiphany on its victim: I could see it in his eyes, come to him clear as a bell the split-second he took his knock—the beggar comprehended physical force's supremacy, its efficiency, the reductive simplicity of its solutions—inferences drawn out of pain, the awful conclusions rolling one after the other, dominoes of logic falling. The new world forced itself upon him: this brand-spanking kakistocracy, an asylum globally administrated by inmates, where God's names were all outlawed and your death began once you'd breached your mother's womb. A punch to the gut and all the fight in him was gone. He searched the brutes' eyes for mercy, or maybe their rationale. The beggar likely saw only the emptiness of violent men: full of idiot nothingness like vultures gorged on roadkill.

"How can I get the money to get her out if I can't even

work?" Tears ran from his eyes. The beggar pleaded. He sounded like a child exhausted from throwing fits. "How can I do any of it if I'm not allowed to do it?"

One of the cops took a black aluminum tire thumper off of his belt. He walloped the beggar over the head. A sickening crack came after; a gushing split through the skull. The cop who'd brained the beggar didn't smile, or emote, or even breathe quicker after bludgeoning his victim. But the other beatcop grinned and squatted down beside the beggar: "You ain't supposed to get her out. You ain't supposed to earn money. You're supposed to do what we say. You're supposed to take it. And, if we let you, you can smile while you eat whole heaping helpings of shit. Don't you know what rolls downhill?" The beatcop followed his admonition with pant-hoots of stupid laughter.

The air smelled of emptying bowels and the metallic-marrow-like stink of spilled human brains. The beggar was no longer listening. The metal tire thumper guaranteed he'd never listen to anything ever again.

The all-black beatcops turned and saw me like I'd just walked onstage into a spotlight. I ran.

The further away I got, the more volubly and louder they laughed. I saw them put a dozen or so boots to the beggar's ribs before I'd got far enough away not to see. The cops punted his ribcage like special teams try-outs. The beggar's head was pink and red and broken. He didn't move other than when he was kicked.

When I was far enough away I told myself I hadn't seen what I had seen. I tried forcing myself to forget by making it something that never happened.

I sprinted through several intersections; I was quickly losing wind and steam. My body was still half-sedated from being laid up in the hospital. I saw all-black beatcops at every corner. They all listened to two-way radios, laughing the way the dumbest animal capable of laughter might laugh, listening through their radios at others laughing the same way. All the mirror-lensed aviators in the world seemed to watch me as I ran.

"He's past due! Ready for collections!" one yelled out. "Send him all the way deep down!" shouted another. I didn't want to know what they meant, but born doomsayers know the sound of doom.

Subjugation, the elimination of personhood. Maybe torture. No, likely torture. That's what they meant. The details could work themselves out later.

———

I saw a door hidden behind an alleyway dumpster. I opened it and ran inside. But my feet found nothing below them. So, I fell—and kept falling—down, down, down, into the deep, deep dark.

I wondered who waited at the bottom.

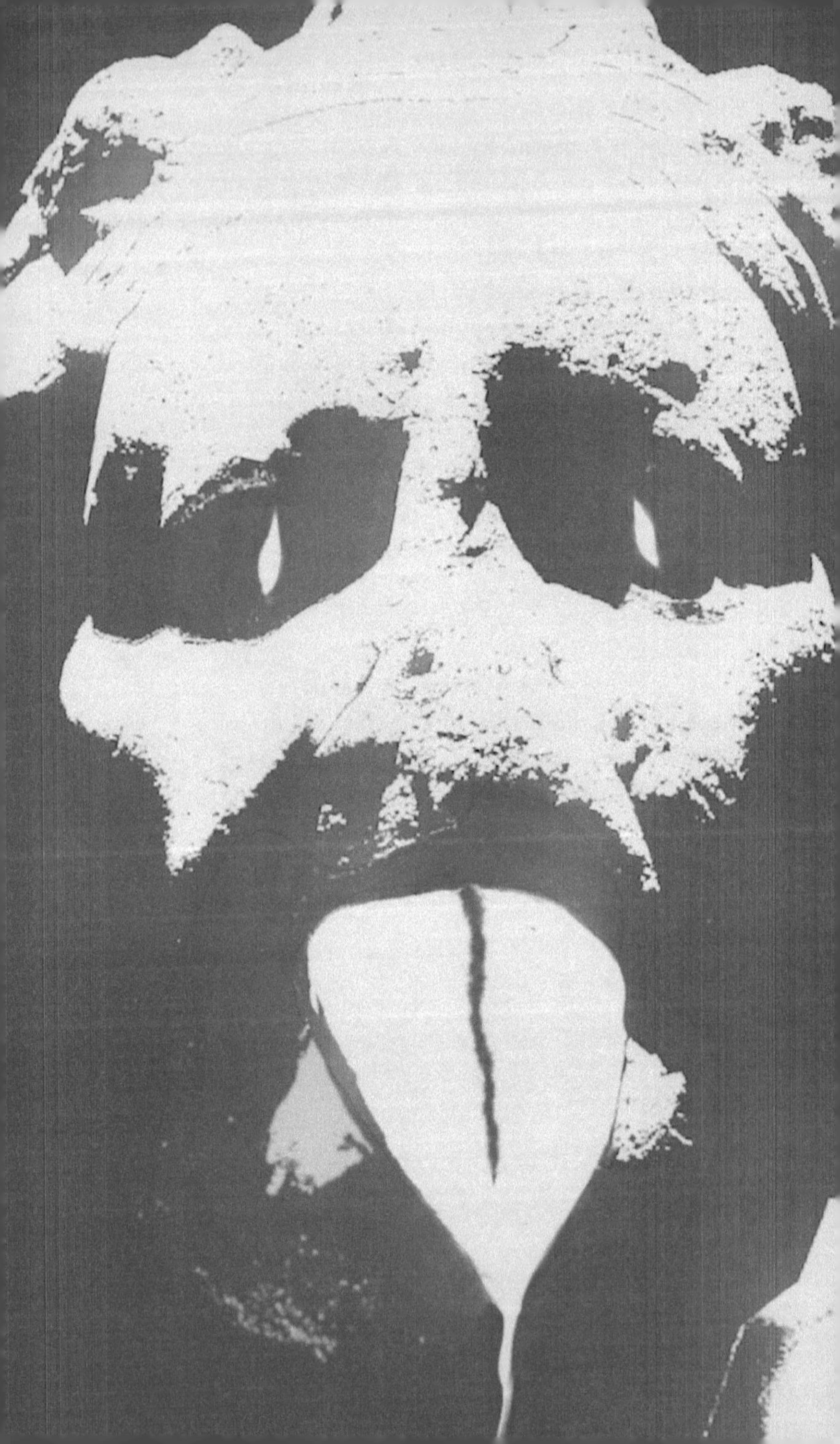

EVER SHALL THEY FEED

I t was a simple if somewhat risky plan. Beno would wait for his father Alvize to break from work and go upstairs for his nightcap and a few menthol cigarettes. During Alvize's stirrup cup smoko, Beno would sneak into the cold room and hide under a sheet on the autopsy slab, lying in wait for his father's return.

You may be wondering why.

Alvize, exercising a habit of masquerading his casual cruelty as good fun, gave a script purportedly "written by Beno" to the student who daily read the morning announcements over the PA system at his son's high school. He gave the same morning announcer forty dollars in cash to ensure that the poem be read. "Beno's Confession" was recited over the PA system at a time when the whole high school's audience was all but guaranteed:

> You know me as Beno, your confederate,
>   confrère
> I disclose you my secret, of which you may
>   not be aware
> To each their arrayed fetishes, all ranked first
>   to last
> And my own favorite fixation? Ogling Mrs.
>   Gulyash's ass

Mrs. Gulyash, the school librarian, was a scoliotic geriatric best known for being shorter than all the students and having night terrors in the middle of the day.

Rather more mean than clever, but there it was.

A bit more color:

While the Gulyashes still lived in Bratislava, Mr. Gulyash, a university professor at Comenius University, ran afoul of the ŠtB (the Czechoslovakian secret police) for the unpardonable crime of reading a passage from the King James Bible to his undergraduate students. Mr. Gulyash was hence found guilty of "subversion of the republic" and sent to Leopoldov State Prison, where he died either having been beaten by the guards, or starved to death by the guards, or otherwise drowning in the unanswerable murk of the police state. Mrs. Gulyash, notwithstanding her "treasonous" defection and the political asylum granted her by the *Američtí brouci* (or, "American bugs") after her husband's dispatch, had long since suffered an unbroken run of rotten luck. After exile from her homeland, she miscarried with her vanished husband's unborn child. Then, there was the retributive campaign against her family by the communist party following her defection, inclusive of her father's ejection from the party (precipitating his fatal heart failure, her mother's consequent Takotsubo's cardiomyopathy soon thereafter, as well as the two resultant funerals she was unable to attend). The apparatchiks even went as far as liquidating the Cesky Terrier breeding operation of her second cousin once removed. This is all to the point that Mrs. Gulyash's lifetime of injury could've done without the added insult of Alvize's lurid verse.

(Not that Alvize had any way of knowing all that. If we're being fair.)

At any rate, the idea of Beno slobbering over Mrs.

Gulyash's hindquarters was judged a real knee-slapper by just about the whole student body. The faculty, too (excepting Mrs. Gulyash, of course).

Enough was enough. This time, the old man was asking for it.

———

It was 8:30 p.m. and Beno was laid up on the slab, covered with a mortuary sheet. And though the cold room was brisk, warmth bloomed in his heart at the thought of his father's comeuppance. The look of fright he imagined he'd see on the old man's face!

For the moment, that was enough to keep his teeth from chattering.

After a short wait, Beno heard the swish and shuffle of his father's loafers move across the floor; he fought the urge to turn and look. Later, he could peek though the accidental eyelet torn through the sheet. When he needed to. When the time was right.

Alvize's footfalls fell nearer the embalming instruments and dissecting tray. Beno thought he might die from anticipation.

What a thought.

Seen through Beno's improvised peephole, his father was backlit by the bright white examination lamps, distinguishable only as shadow fringed in light. Beno readied himself and, not having picked his moment so much as his moment having picked him, got ready to jump-scare the old man from under the sheet.

But before he could, the unexpected, beady ratchet of a yanked pull chain stalled him out. And, at seeing his father's figure better-revealed by the chain's attached light,

Beno could at last feel the bitter briskness of the cold room.

Beno didn't understand what he was looking at. Why would his father be naked? But, obviously, there he was, stood between the two autopsy tables in his age-spotted birthday suit. And still in his penny loafers.

Beno did not know what his father was doing. He also did not know what he himself should do now. Funny how just one thing sends the whole world topsy-turvy.

Or maybe it was not funny at all. Suppose it must be a matter of perspective.

———

ALVIZE PICKED THE SCALPEL UP OFF THE DISSECTING TRAY. He pulled the sheet off of Mrs. Bernuzzi's corpse.

By all accounts, the living Bernuzzi had had a reputation. The intimate details of which, of course, would soon be forthcoming. What he hadn't already heard from other corpses' hearsay, he'd extract from Bernuzzi's soon enough.

Once he'd done feeding Mother Ghoul.

She who, upon being fed, fed him in turn. Suckling her teat, he'd drink up the secrets her tongue had read from lifeless flesh. In death, the human body spoke, if one but learned to listen.

Alvize examined Mrs. Bernuzzi's nude cadaver, and was satisfied with his work; the flaying, methodical, the slices deft and precise, incised as if by the hands of a surgeon, leaving neither contractures nor adhesions.

He sliced into Carolina Bernuzzi's thigh with his scalpel, taking up where he'd left off. Pulling away a pearly strip glistening with fascia, he shuddered, feeling the satisfaction of competency, the higher purpose that only the true craftsman can feel.

———

BENO THOUGHT MAYBE SOMEONE WAS FORCING HIS FATHER to do what he was doing. There were such analogues, he reasoned, in both fact and fiction; men coopted into political assassination under the threat of execution, women who married scoundrels to pay off parents' debts. There were in fact whole storybooks full of deeds done under duress.

Maybe there was a shadowy cabal instigating this mutilative freakery, or even some singular bad actor, a renegade lunatic forcing his father, for some reason, to desecrate this woman's corpse. Because the alternative was unacceptable. The notion that Alvize had himself chosen, of his own free will, to strip off his clothes, and further, to strip the flesh off a dead woman, was laden with a psychological freight too damaging for Beno to carry himself.

And why was the old man still wearing his loafers?

A thousand troubling thoughts bombarded Beno in his foxhole; he squeezed the whole of himself shut against their intrusion. He stopped up his airway, and bore down on his gut, and shut up his eyes, as if his father's perversions threatened to invade not only Beno's mind but his body. But the more tightly he tried to rein in his intrusive thoughts, the more wildly they ran riot; Beno envisioned sex games and necrophilia, cannibalism and human sacrifice, violently enacted heathen black rites. A slew of frightening sacrileges.

His mind was broken by his father's sins, whether real or imagined, and by Beno's fears, untamable creatures unto themselves.

At a point he understood he couldn't hold his breath

much longer than he had. So he let air in his lungs and his bodily tension loose. And when he did, the deathly clinic wrapped him in its frigid silence, and Beno, breathing in the cold quiet, soon realized: his father was no longer in the room.

———

Alvize continued down stone stairs and through underground corridors, carrying meat packageable by the pound. The walls perspired sog, sweating the deep damp of earth from their mineral pores.

She waited in the dungeon's utmost tenebrosity. Tallow candles melted into puddles of wax, smelled of rancid beef and butter, pooling around the morbidity of her morbid obesity, the creature herself looking somewhat to have melted. Flames danced over her tumorous growths that were like dripping lumps of lard, her skin sallow and sweat-slickened under the light.

She was a heap of saddlebagged adipose. Mother Ghoul and the melted tallow looked like they might blend.

Rats scurried around her in a frenzy, fur patchy and balding from mange, flea-bitten ears budded with lesions, dried blood barnacled all over their tails. Their bodies, swollen and fat; two, maybe three times fatter and longer than wharf rats. Hearing Alvize enter the room, they shrieked and capered across Mother Ghoul's humps.

Whether in excitement or fear, Alvize never could tell.

———

Beno's Adam's apple bobbed in the dry catch of his

throat. His lips trembled. What was this place, hidden behind and below the family funeral home walls?

His cellphone flashlight lit up the stone passage, moist with lichenous exudate. It was like walking through an ecological chest cold. Primitive symbols, chiseled into the walls, eroded by damp and time. The ceiling raftered with speleothems, a canker-sored mineral mouth. A frieze depicted scenes of man-sized rats feasting on flesh, of rat-like humans doing the same.

A liquid orange light glowed up ahead in the dark, and he quickly shut off the screen on his phone. A reeking, fatty smoke smacked him on the nose. He heard vermin shrill and skitter, premonition darkly working itself inside him, throbbing all the way deep down in his bones.

At that, Beno confronted the paradox of his disposition:

He knew he would not stop himself from seeing what he did not want to see.

———

"I want living flesh next time," Mother Ghoul said. Abscesses punctured her jowls, oozing an organic black tar through perforated skin. The holes in her face were wide enough to show microbial cultures cultivating themselves on her too-sharp teeth. Her eyes looked strange under the dizzy flicker of the flames, blighted the black and yellow of a bruised and rotten lemon.

"I know, Mother," Alvize said.

"And the children are hungry for living flesh, too."

"Yes, I know. I am doing what I can."

Mother Ghoul harrumphed.

"May I feed you?" he asked.

She might've kept carping, but as it was, she was

starved. Alvize dangled Bernuzzi's meat over Mother Ghoul's maw. She chuffed and snouted at the fresh-cut flesh, waggling her greedy tongue. She looked like a killer whale nipping herring from a trainer's hand.

A rat resembling a Scottish Terrier in shape and size leapt for the dangling meat. Alvize threw an elbow into its mutant jaw; the dog-rat scuttered while flying through the air. Maybe it meant to hit the ground running. Instead, it cracked the back of its skull against the sharp edge of a stone.

The vicious hit hardly drew Mother's notice.

"I am mindful of your hunger. I have not forgotten your hunger, and I am, as always, eager to satisfy it," Alvize said.

"Yes, so long as you're a beneficiary. You rent-seeker. You forget, Alvize, my longevity. When you're rotting in your bed of worms, perhaps I'll savor your son in a stew. Mind that you treat me well!"

These threats, all old hat. "I only urge caution, Mother. Only caution." Alvize dipped a strip of cadaver down into her mouth. "The world is changing. Feeding isn't so simple as it was. It's a world of eyes now; eyes everywhere and in everything. An electric society of peeping Toms. There is a permanent audience of interlopers, watching, always. We must guard ourselves against them."

She slurped the meat onto her tongue to gnash between her needled teeth. Phlegm percolated her sinuses, bubbled as she chewed. Alvize didn't understand how her lips could smack so loudly.

"Flesh—I want living flesh!" Gobbets of graying meat spat out as she spoke.

These had been trying years, these last, spent skirting the exposure of digitalia's creeping kingdom. How could Alvize keep pace with Mother Ghoul's hunger, intensifying as it did with every feeding? How could they keep hiding, in this day and age?

And then the rats. Yes, the rats…

Growing larger, ever larger, killing each other and eating themselves, now more often than not refusing the whole barrels of rendered meat Alvize brought to feed them. They'd grown hungrier than their gruesome matron for the pulsating flavor of living things.

And the scarcity of human flesh, and the hunger that that scarcity could not fill, meant Mother Ghoul often would not, sometimes even could not, share her visions with him, no matter how desperate Alvize was for a fix of her peculiar narcotic.

But it was something that he had to have. Nothing titillated like the secrets of the crypt. Reliving the hidden shame that outlasted the bodies of the dead—that scopophilic pleasure was only Mother Ghoul's to give.

She'd finished her last morsel. A sigh preceded a series of pungent eructations. "I suppose you'll want your fill now, too?"

Alvize's body yearned for Mother's milk; he drew in toward her, a brittle vine crawling over a bleak house toward the black sun. Always, such burning shame in his longing. Always.

"Yes," he quietly said.

Mother Ghoul sinisterly smiled.

———

BENO WAS ROOTED TO THE DIRT FLOOR OF THE CATACOMB, legs somehow syrupy and heavy as lead all at once, fingers tingled numb and insensibly gripping the rocky edge ringing the chamber's secret entry. He kept his body behind the rocks' formations but his eyes hidden in plain sight.

He did not yet understand what he was watching—or was perhaps unable to understand, given the perversity such as comprehension required—though his brain interpreted the visual data clearly, cataloging in detail every foul act:

A hugely fat woman—mountain of gristly drippings atop a sloppy mound of meat. Her fissured face wept a foul-smelling resin, teeth like rust-smeared awls peeking through unanatomical holes. Her eyes were grimy yellow-black. The stink invaded Beno so deeply that the stench curled around his ears before being sucked inside his skull.

Beno watched her ugly-fat fingers lift up her gut, his living parent supine on the ground, sinking into mud, naked as the day he was born (but for his penny loafers). The old man's eyes were glassy orbs filled with liquid fire, two pools ignited while spilling over with fuel. Alvize stared up at the spiny dark.

And then, from the stink of her greasy marsupium, there emerged a protuberance. A wretched limb.

It looked like a forearm with an elbow where there was supposed to be a hand, a nipple enclosing the elbow. It dribbled something bituminous, black tinged midnight-green, liquid spikes rippling above the surface. Like a dripping roll of razor wire unbundling itself.

Then, horribly, oh so horribly, the malformed limb lowered, so the nipple extended over Alvize's mouth. His lips puckered and his tongue folded into a papillary envelope, lapping at the air as the nipple descended down between his teeth, and—

———

—Alvize suckled Bernuzzi's chronicle of closest-kept secrets from Mother's freakish tit. And soon Alvize was so light, so, so light that he felt himself floating off somewhere, as a driven leaf, almost weightless on the wind. Alvize became the unliving Bernuzzi, wallowing inside her ghost in fragments of her past:

Alvize was Bernuzzi, snorting cocaine in a dingy bathroom while disco pounded outside the toilet stall door; he was Bernuzzi, swilling bottom-shelf gin before passing out on the bathroom floor; Bernuzzi, stamping scarlet letters on tramps who traipsed up the corporate ladder in increments of spread legs. Alvize was Bernuzzi, using a wooden spoon to beat her mentally-disabled son for not turning down the TV, spiking her whorish niece's coffee with levonorgestrel to flush out her bastard baby, kicking her ex-husband's dog with her high heel's spike, poisoning the mutt three weeks later, habitually spitting in patrons' side salads and soups, drunkenly wheeling into a child pedestrian in a witnessless hit-and-run—

Oh what tender-sweet sins had blossomed from this awful woman!

Of course, Alvize had had a feeling. His sense of depravity was keenly developed from experience in the field.

And then, when he'd drank his fill, he lay completely still, on the floor between Mother Ghoul's feet, struggling to remain a ghost in Bernuzzi's terrible memories, which to him were like shameful dreams of ecstasy.

He did not want to let go.

Beno ran. Oh, how quickly Beno ran.

———

BENO HAD NEVER BEFORE NOTICED HOW LOW THE LAMP hung over the kitchen table. How feeble the light glowed beneath the pendant's stained-glass shade. How its sparse luminance extinguished itself before the dusty table's edge. Never before had he noticed the accumulations of grot and gunge, or seen neglection's texture wearing down the woodgrain, the spalting like veins overcome with decay.

Had he really never noticed? Truly never *seen*?

This wasn't a kitchen; it was an incubator of filth. A monument to dilapidation. One dead lightbulb had been there the better part of three years. He recognized the smoky stain of the blown filament on the glass bulb, burnt in the shape of a comic book speech bubble.

His dead mother's nicked and notched porcelain plates glowered over him with blank faces frowning chipped teeth, as hungry as they were dumb. Beno supposed that he could say that about many things.

Perhaps it was better that his mother was dead.

Had Beno's mother known? Was Alvize's perversion begun before her final season? Had she known? How could she not have? Was his mother the mother of his gauzy memory, model of good will and cheer, exemplar of physical hygiene and spiritual cleanliness? Or was she an agent of dereliction, part of this sickness and slime? What was her part in their home's dissolution?

"You're not eating," Alvize said to Beno. "Oatmeal's no good?"

"Huh?" Beno looked up, having only half-heard what his father said.

"I said, is the oatmeal no good?"

Beno shook his head. "No, no, it's fine. I'm just thinking

about a project for school…" Beno regretted breathing this place's foul funk. "Need some time to look it over before class." He checked his watch despite knowing the time.

"You'd better get going, then, huh?" Alvize said.

Beno looked up at his father. Milk dripped over Alvize's lower lip and down his chin. Was the dribble midnight-green? A dying lightbulb guttered, barely surviving the blink, then shone hotly bright, its evaporating filament about to arc and explode. But it didn't. Beno saw the milk run from his father's mouth was an uncorrupted white.

But without a steady light always shining, how could Beno really know?

"Beno," his father said.

Beno didn't want to speak anymore, not to his father, not to anyone. Maybe not for a very long time. There was a rage he'd never known was sleeping deep down in his soul, now awoken by his doubts. Fury seized him, choked him, blurred the world around him. He'd break the goddamn rotten table and smash the broken lights. He would—

"Beno," his father said.

"Yeah?"

"I'm sorry." Alvize stirred his cereal. He managed to look Beno in the eyes before diverting back to his spoon. "About the morning announcements. I went too far."

"You went too far," Beno repeated what his father said. He could feel the words' shapes and sounds but they bore no communicative properties. Beno understood the human tongue as an instrument of meaninglessness, of noise and nothing more. The world was not what it was.

"Yes, yes, I did." Alvize set his spoon down by his bowl, milk pooling around the head of the spoon. Beno wondered if the milk would turn to spoil the table, or if the already-spoiled table would contaminate the milk. Where did the rot begin? And where did it end? Did it ever end at all?

"I thought you would think it was funny," Alvize said, "but now I realize it was childish and hurtful." He pleached his fingers and attempted paternal warmth. "Do you forgive me?"

Beno looked at his watch again. He didn't look back up. "Sure."

"Good. Good, good." Alvize's eyes flicked back and forth between the table and the boy. "Then—then, I guess, have a good day."

"Have a good day."

Beno picked up his bag to leave for school. On his way out, he saw his father's loafers set out beside the door. He newly grasped something he'd surely long since known; his father had always sat bare-footed at their kitchen table. Beno decided that rhyme and reason, in footwear or otherwise, were features of a former life.

————

Mother Ghoul wondered if Alvize knew his son had seen them.

There was no longer any pressing need for Alvize to bring her anything but dead flesh. As matters now stood, they could no longer stand. She needed the meat hot, still pulsating, livid with pain and sensation. That was what she wanted—no, *deserved*—to eat.

Once there were such unholy days of glory…

She could sift the grains of every forepassed life with oracular precision. But she was not in fact an oracle, could only see the secrets still hidden in the past. No, she could not divine those events still to come.

And who knew what the unknown future might bring? Perhaps the boy would deliver where Alvize came up short. One day, perhaps. In any event, all things in their own good time. Even those things that crawl in the dark.

Every Mother's son was extended an open invitation. And, maybe—maybe every Mother's son would one day come home.

One of the mammoth rats bit her swollen ankle. She smiled and let it eat. It was only natural for hungry children to feed.

———

Arriving at school, Beno saw Mrs. Gulyash walking in from the teacher's lot. While hobbling across the zebra stripe and onto the school sidewalk, she spotted him, too. Mrs. Gulyash waved to Beno. And Beno waved back.

People weren't who other people thought they were. Nobody was.

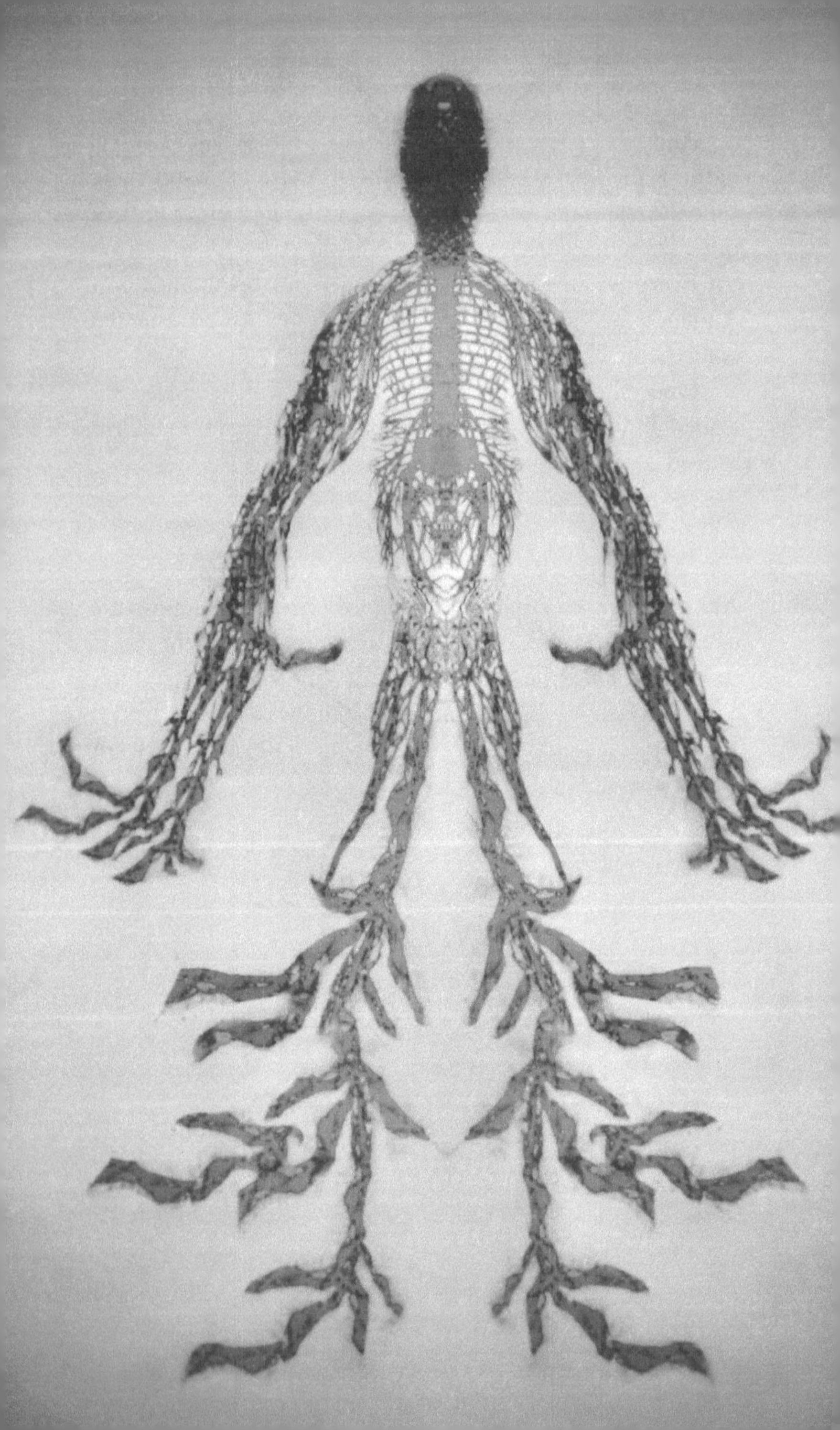

EGUISTO ZANOSI'S FAST

Dinner at Saint Theo's. Nikki, dressed in a black cocktail dress and micro-grid fishnet stockings, glittery Jimmy Choo knockoff pumps. Eguisto thought she looked like a high-class escort. It put a nice bow on his Madonna-whore complex.

He pawed at her crotch under the table, smeared prosciutto-greased fingers on her dress, left house red in puddles all over the tablecloth. By the time he paid the check, the waitstaff were glowering at him like a houseguest caught sleeping in junior's crib.

Nikki went down on him in the taxi. He would have finished if he hadn't caught the cabbie staring through the rearview.

Now Eguisto waited in Nikki's bed, in her dingy squat overtop an Indian restaurant in Murray Hill. She couldn't afford paid streaming, so he watched *How It's Made*, ads and all, while she conducted her precoital sacraments in the john. The episode was about pinball machines. Pretty interesting stuff, actually.

He heard the toilet bowl lid slam violently shut. Then the shower curtain rings snapped off all at once.

"You alright?" No answer. "Nikki?"

Eguisto got up off the bed, a draft slipping through the pre-war windows to bite the tips of his toes. He went and stood outside the bathroom door. A somewhat fecal odor drifted over, a whiff of spoiled garlic and rotten eggs.

"Nikki? Did you fall?"

He meant to knock. Until he heard something like a meat mallet pounding a juicy steak. At that, a vestigial, prehistoric fear put him off of rapping on the door. Eguisto heard slopping footfalls, like someone tromping through mud and muck. He heard a gargantuan stomach's excretive growl.

The indwelling caveman of his subconscious demanded a full retreat.

"Hey Nikki, I just remembered, I'm picking my cousin up at LaGuardia." He quickly started dressing. "Rain check, though. I'll call you later, okay?"

Eguisto didn't wait for an answer.

He had neither the time nor presence of mind amidst his flight to notice the watery black ink seeping into the bedroom's carpet from under the bathroom door.

He fled Nikki's apartment still holding his shoes.

———

A BOWL OF *NERO DE SEPPIA* WAITED FOR HIM ON THE KITCHEN island at home. Pasta dyed black with cuttlefish ink was, to the very visual Eguisto, the highest of high gastronomy (along with escargot and tongue).

Beside the bowl, there was a note:

"A last meal, for your limitless appetite. I love you, Eggie, but you have no self-control. I'm going to my mother's. I don't know when I'll be home."

His wretched mother-in-law, Mirella Straulino, lived in the Mount Zoncolan foothills in Sutrio. A Friulian backwater, where they hardly even spoke Italian. Well, Lina's stepfather Pieri supposedly spoke English (though Eguisto was skeptical, the man never talked). Truth be told, Lina's parents gave Eguisto the creeps. Not least because Pieri's left hand was missing all its fingers—probably lopped off slaughtering chickens, or fooling around with that guillotine the crackpots kept in their wine cellar—not to mention Mirella roaming the arboretum naked by moonlight. The Straulino *casale* was a weird place inhabited by weird people. Eguisto was all too relieved when their weeklong visit was done.

Is that where Lina meant she was going?

Eguisto called his wife's cell. It went straight to voicemail without ringing.

"Shit."

Not knowing what to do, he went back to the kitchen.

At least he had something to eat.

———

Eguisto tossed and turned, and sweated through his sheets.

He dreamt of Roscoe, his family's little Manchester Terrier, chasing rats inside the fence of their Jewel Streets slum. That backwater boulevard of dying industry, nestled in the ghettoized coastal floodplain their neighbors called The Hole. Eguisto once called that place home.

He dreamt of Roscoe running circuits on the yard, hunting vermin in a frenzy, whipping rats around like ragdolls until their necks finally went *snap!*

He dreamt a dark rogue wave rising from the Atlantic, almost a hundred feet high. An ink-black tsunami cresting over Jamaica Bay before crashing into Howard Beach and roaring toward The Hole.

———

EGUISTO WOKE UP TO FIND HE'D VOMITED UP HIS DINNER. IT covered almost his entire bed, like he'd fallen asleep in a swale of blackly congealing crude oil.

———

"I'M JUST SAYING, IT'S A LITTLE PREMATURE TO WORRY about Lina cutting you off. You're not there quite yet." Trent Kyŏng speared a piece of *tamagoyaki*, bit a chunk of egg off the end of his chopstick. Once Eguisto's college roommate, he was now a cutthroat divorce attorney complete with well-heeled clientele.

Eguisto nipped at his sake, nervously bouncing his knee. "You tell that to your clients? 'Don't worry about it'?"

"You're not my client. I start talking to you like a client —that's how you know you're in trouble." Trent noticed Eguisto hadn't touched his sashimi. "What's the matter? I thought this was your joint. *Maguro*'s no good?"

Eguisto groaned. "Lina made pasta last night. It didn't agree with me."

Trent wiped his mouth with his napkin, shaking his head. "You cheat on your wife, and she still cooks you dinner. Eggie, buddy."

"Yeah?"

"Ever heard the saying, 'Shape up or ship out'?"

Eguisto rubbed the heel of his hand against his brow. "Once or twice," he said, his eyes twitching.

"Ever tried?"

"I'm working up to it."

"You don't get it, Eggie. Playtime's over. Balling out some side piece isn't a flex. It just means you're a mess. Vide

Billy Shakes, pal. I can smell your Danish kingdom rotting. You picking up what I'm putting down?"

Eguisto waved off his friend. He sucked his teeth and looked away.

"Pal. You're headed the way of your old man. A dried-out old coozehound, collecting SSI, EBT—the whole alphabet soup. Bedding down in a double-wide with your toothless fuckbuddy, Miss Methany—can't make rent and got nowhere else to go."

"T, you know, you're a real laugh riot."

"Eggie." Trent leaned stony-eyed overtop of the table. "Who's laughing?"

After that, Eguisto drank in silence.

———

SEVERAL DAYS PASSED, WITH EGUISTO'S HUNGER EVOLVING actual starvation. At swallowing the meagerest portion, his body (explosively) vomited it all back out. In desperation, he tested international cuisine's whole bill of fare, buying every exotic ingredient from every third-world grocery, funneling a global horn of plenty right down his trap. No matter the meal, Eguisto couldn't keep down a crumb.

His blood sugar dropped. Moving between rooms brought on dizzy spells. Total fatigue drained his bodily battery dead. By nighttime, he was moribund, his muscles aching and bloodless, teetering closer to mortal deficit.

Maybe he was dying. Minimally, redline catabolic. Christ, he'd eat cockroaches if he could.

Lina's phone actually rang now when he called her.

But she still wouldn't answer.

———

Eguisto realized by the fourth day of his involuntary fast that if he didn't go to a hospital soon, he wouldn't be able to go at all.

It might've already been too late.

Because the second he left his apartment at The Gansvort, he stumbled into vertigo. Disequilibrium steepened at every uncertain step. Motor control short-circuiting, he crashed just outside his building.

The doorman, Gómez, caught him by his elbow. "Mr. Zanosi, you okay?" He steadied Eguisto at his elbow and back. "You don't look so hot."

"I'm fine," he said, catching his breath, politely trying to wave Gómez away. "I'm fine."

"Should I call someone?"

"No, no. No, I'm—"

Eguisto froze.

Lina.

She was standing there, just across the street. And dressed—how best to describe it? Frumpily. Outfitted in an all-black blouse, apron dress, and shawl. Dressed, as a matter of fact, just like her mother.

Lina's lips dripped ink-black drool. She was grinning a lunatic's grin.

"Lina!"

Gómez grabbed for Eguisto, but missed getting a handhold by a fraction of an inch. Still waving to his wife, the starved lover blindly jaywalked across Christopher Street.

And right in front of an oncoming car.

———

Eguisto opened his eyes to the sanitized white light

of a hospital ward. His hunger was now supernatural—like crucifixion, an agony only relievable by God or death.

Attempting to talk, he discovered he'd been intubated. Soft restraints tethered Eguisto to the hospital bed. A chemical drip blanketed him in its muzzy sedation.

Two female doctors pushed in past his privacy curtain. Each wore a jet-colored widow's veil draped down to their shoulders, obscuring their faces and necks.

"*Siet sigûr?*" An old woman's voice—not quite Italian, but a close kindred tongue.

"*Sì. Lui o darìn di mangiâ cumò,*" the younger one said.

Thereupon both women were unveiled by cryptic transmutation, their shrouds dissipating in airy drifts of black vapor. Lina and her mother Mirella's faces materialized therethrough; a bolt out of the blue, but no less inevitable for it. Viscous black sludge oozed through their teeth, staining their smiles dreadful.

Lina came close and held Eguisto's hand. Fool that he was, he thought she meant to soothe him. No. She pried his left pinky away from his other fingers by force, then pressed that digit down against his hospital bed's railing.

Eguisto could be slow on the uptake, but by now he recognized something was off.

Mirella plucked a stiletto from beneath her white coat while joining her daughter beside Eguisto. While the endotracheal tube obstructed his vocal cords, he was unable to scream, though it was not for lack of trying. He thrashed and he bucked, desperately trying to escape. But the IV's narcotic drip diluted his strength.

Medievally brutal pain attended the stiletto's amputation of his pinky. Lina caught Eguisto's severed finger in her hand as her mother finished cutting.

His wife held his endotracheal tube near where the

connector attached the ventilator circuit, while Mirella touched her knife to his jugular vein.

"If you scream," Lina said, "*Mamé* will slit your throat. Understood?"

Tears trickled down around his runny nose. Eguisto nodded; yes, he understood.

Lina extubated him with the delicacy of a pediatric nurse. Then both women coldly watched him weep in quiet for a while.

"Are you calm now?" Lina eventually said.

Eguisto felt pathetically childlike answering, "Yes."

"And still hungry?"

He nodded.

"Open your mouth," Lina said, and held out his amputated finger.

Eguisto stared a good, long while at Lina. He hesitated, then shook his head, and eventually said, "No."

"*Menaçâ di tirâi vie i testicui,*" Lina said to her mother.

Mirella brought her stiletto within alarming proximity of his testicles.

"Open your mouth, or *Mamé* will cut off your balls."

Tears passed his trembling lips as they parted. Lina set Eguisto's pinky down on his tongue. Then, pushing up against his chin, she helped close his mouth for him. "Chew."

Mirella menaced Eguisto again, reminding him of her knife.

He began consuming himself.

"Try, if you can, swallowing every last bite."

———

At length, Eguisto gnawed through his finger's meat to collagen and bone.

"Spit," Lina said, holding an expectant palm below his chin. "Let's see."

Eguisto gobbed out a drool of bloody bones into her hand. He'd barely left the gristle.

Lina, much pleased with herself, chirruped as she tucked her husband's liberated finger in her pocket. "Now," she said, "are you feeling better?"

Eguisto's dizzy emptiness subsided. His body was reinvigorated; felt full of fresh, new blood. Yes, in fact, he did feel very much better. Indeed, his grievous hunger now seemed all but gone. "I feel better," he said, brimming over with tears. "I feel better."

Mirella held the bloody knife up to the bright surgical lights and, staring starry-eyed at the incarnadine blade, growled the low, loud growl of a very big man. "*Mangjâ di te stes se no tu sês jemplât de porzion de tô vite!*"

"Eat only of yourself if you are not filled with your life's portion," Lina said (presumably in translation). Her deeds had painted her face in a ghoulish, black-toothed grin.

After gently kissing Eguisto's lips, she unfastened his restraints.

"Come, *gno amôr*, it's time to go home."

"Yes, dear."

"*Mamé* will cook something now that you're well again. You'll need your energy—a thousand things to do, as many places to see. Did you know this is *Mamé*'s first time in New York City?"

IF PROMISES WERE MEANT TO KEEP

In Lurcu's Gate, men are less than men. They are amounts.

Penal colonies are by their nature levelers of person-hood. Numerating places. They value integers of sentence length, sequences of prisoner identification. Even prisoners' black-market brokerage is tolerated in certain amounts, if the exchange is anticipated and, more importantly, quantified.

An oppressive regime of numbers. Quantification's insidious rule, as petty as angry church ladies seeing pretty little girls. A bodiless dictator, reigning in enumerative tyranny. And who are we, if not enumeration's living casualties? Once named men, now reduced to ledger columns. Our memorialization, in black ink, and zeroes, and nothing more. The numerical indexing of the propertyless, the choiceless, the hopeless.

Quantity is erasure's sine qua non. A seeming paradox, I know.

———

THERE IS ALWAYS A STORY BEFORE THE STORY BEGINS.

There was a man who arrived here in adolescence, as early in life as any other inmate ever has. "Tiny" Buček. He was a giant, his legacy imparted by hard labor's accumulations upon his lengthy frame. Contrarily named for the sake of cheek, as giants often are.

In this place a man dies two deaths, the spirit preceding the body. We thought Tiny the exception. He was, only he was the exception that proved the rule.

Tiny was sent up the river patsy in a frame-up job, catching an all-day bid for murder. Before that, only a boy, a peasant of Austria-Hungary's Slovene territories, fleeing its imperium before poverty could dig his rut. I knew little of him, littler of his home, and of his crime not much more. Penologically speaking, foreigners are serviceable stand-ins for natives. That I knew, and that was enough.

A reduction of Tiny's tenure in this hell: Endured through three wardens, thirty-seven winters, and seven failed escapes. Shot by two guards, fourteen teeth lost, all ten of his fingers (twice) denailed with pliers. He'd claimed an acquaintance with seven different ghosts (whether phantoms of the ether or his imagination, I really can't say).

Tiny habitually marked a tree trunk to record his sentence's daily increments. The judge decreed Buček's term should outlast his expiry, and so the tally grew. Tiny's register covered half of the bark. And at last tally, the Everlasting Tiny Buček had abided thirteen-thousand, six-hundred and ninety-two days and nights without freedom's reprieve.

It ought to have seemed inevitable that Tiny would live to see his tree destroyed. Maybe he never considered the possibility. He was unprepared when the guards chopped his memorial down. Tiny consequently suffered a deep psychological fracture. A complete mental and spiritual disintegration, in fact.

Tiny left this place before his body. Lights turned on, nobody home.

Tiny Buček, survivor of the oceans of bondage, at last swallowed by the Penitentiary Sea. And if he could be devoured, then the rest of us?

Krill. We are like krill.

———

I WAS ONCE MARRIED TO GALA ECKORD. YOU, AND ANYONE else alive at the dawn of the twentieth century, will know her by her stage name.

Gala Borner.

You'll ask if I mean *the* Gala Borner. Am I talking about the sultress who lit up the Astor, the Knickerbocker, the New Amsterdam, and every stage in between? That shooting starlet streaking every blockbuster playbill? The one who outshone the blue bloods on the society page? Am I saying she was my wife?

The very same.

It is a remarkable and bittersweet truth that, yes, Gala Borner and I once belonged to one another.

No more.

I was convinced she was running around on me. And what was my proof? Well, of course there was none. Drunks are as unparticular as to evidence as they are picky for their poison. We're hateful, small people; every one of us, to a flask-bearing man.

I was not jealous or vindictive when I was sober, but a demon in my cups. The problem being, you might've guessed, that I was always in my cups. Always, always.

As Gala's star ascended, and the money flooded in (a deluge, in fact, and more than the two of us could ever hope to spend), every glass I drank was bottomless. I had easements on barstools in every gin mill in the city.

When I wasn't tumbling hooch in speakeasies, I lived with Gala in The Osborne, catty-cornered to Carnegie Hall. Swanky place that it was, too.

We resided in the precinct of the younger Cornelius Vanderbilt's château, whose peak overthrew the spire of nearby Saint Thomas Church. Not quite spitting distance, but two blocks to Fifth Avenue cut close enough. Cornie Junior even stopped Gala on the street once, told her she made Cléo de Mérode look like a toad.

For a while, life could be like that. A real pip.

She entranced the men who minted the Gilded Age and the progressives eager to bury it. She gabbed with princesses as if born to the purple, got chummy with down-and-outers like the girl from the tenement next door. To me, she was everything. And then, sometimes, she was nothing. Or something worse than nothing. My scapegoat; a monster. Sometimes I couldn't stand to not be with her; sometimes I couldn't stand to be with her at all.

"If you go out on me, I'll kill you," is what I used to say.

And her answer was always the same:

"For promises we'll only weep, if promises were meant to keep."

Hell if I knew what it meant. Gala was a dotty gal.

Her being gone, now there's nothing to me, except that I'm better-known than most other murderers. (Because of my victim, you understand. I've no claim to fame of my own.) You know what kind of man is known only in his infamy?

A ghoul.

I don't need to read the tea leaves; I'll die in Lurcu's Gate, this I already know. And I don't need to be told I deserve to.

I know that, too.

———

Good black humor is a matter of distance. If you're stepping on the executioner's toes, you're too close for a real knee-slapper. Us inmates meant for the drop were consequently disinclined to taking the piss, the shadows of the gallows stretched too far over us to indulge in gallows humor.

"Eck, they're coming." Jacob the embezzler spoke with a harsh bite of urgency. He and I were friendly in the way of dogs who raid refuse bins together after a month foraging the same dead-end street.

Whereupon came the guards.

Not guards of any official stamp, but our labor camp's capos. These were the ones who backstabbed their way to a bounty amidst famine to which only vultures ever obtain. Scavengers, survivalists. The men who, if the world ended, would live to rebuild.

A sobering notion.

"Eckord. You're due in the infirmary." I looked up to find Carlu, the capos' captain, standing over me. Carlu was missing most of his teeth and all of his conscience. He frightened me much more than his sizable henchman, Bingo, whose congenital dullness made him more livestock than man. An ox is domesticable, psychopaths notoriously less so.

That Bingo at that moment broke wind, and then, surprised by his own flatulence, swiveled his head toward that very sound he'd produced, was unremarkable. It was well-known that his mental capacity was limited to the threshold of his brainstem. Bingo was, in fact, convicted for burglarizing his hometown's chief of police. Stupid didn't begin to describe him. How that imbecile thought he could get away with anything, big and dumb as he was, I don't know.

"Where?" I said.

"The infirmary," Carlu repeated. "You're wanted in the infirmary."

"We have an infirmary?"

Jacob leaned in toward me and whispered, "The abandoned chicken coop."

I still didn't understand.

"The Torture Hutch," Jacob said.

I turned to consult our severally toothless captain.

"Yeah," Carlu said, "the Torture Hutch."

———

I'D NEVER BEEN IN THE COOP. IT SEEMED AN UNLIKELY VENUE for strappado and the water cure (whose torments were suffered by no small number of inmates, but not yet by me). But if I've ever been surprised along the calaboose's learning curve, it's due my delusions of remnant humanity. Which, of course, did not pertain in Lurcu's Gate. This coop and colony both housed animals. So, yes, I realized, the Torture Hutch made perfect sense.

"Sit," Warden Smiker said. He was attired in military dinner dress and gold spectacles. He looked like a schoolteacher dressed for a costume ball.

I took the wooden stool across the desk from Smiker while he fussed over stacks of forms and papers. His banker's lamp shone over a desk full of them, like a shabby drafting table for fabricating cryptograms. An oxblood-colored fountain pen flew from his hand over the forms.

"Inmate Eckord," he said without looking up, closely attending his penal bureaucracy's documentation, "it is the policy of the Lurcu's Gate Penal Colony to offer, from time to time, a special clemency to select inmates."

Smiker looked up. In his spectacle lenses' reflection, I saw one of his household orderlies just behind me, carrying a serving tray with a cloche-covered plate. Smiker nodded. The orderly entered into my lefthand field of vision, then set the tray down on Smiker's desk in front of where I sat.

Steam vented from the seam between the cloche and plate, dispersing an aroma of seared meat and greens, smelling ungodly good. I'd underestimated Warden Smiker. Truly, the man knew how psychological sadism worked.

"We are considering you for this special clemency," Smiker said.

There was a medieval head crusher stored in a nesting box nearby. "Clemency?" I said.

Smiker located a form with my photograph paper-clipped to the upper lefthand corner. He faced me directly and held my record up along his line of sight, comparing me to my likeness. "You're the wife-killer, yes?"

I flinched. The sobriquet that never loses its sting.

"The famous actress," Smiker said. "What was her name?"

"Gala Borner, sir."

Smiker snapped his fingers and nodded into his chest. "That's right. Gala Borner." He paused, likely firming up the association. Then, returned to his forms.

The orderly removed the cloche from the plate. *Côte de boeuf bordelaise* and *haricots verts*, cooked as in the Café des Beaux Arts, that Bustanoby Brothers' joint where Gala and I so often ate. A caramelized crust on a juicy ribeye, the green beans drowned in butter sauté; a smell to make a man delirious. Could've knocked me over with a feather.

But that's the trick of torment, isn't it? The warden,

contrary to my earliest inkling, was an innovator of torture's discipline.

The orderly set down a tin wine tumbler and held a bottle out for me to inspect. I looked at the label. A tawny Kopke port. I had once bought a whole case of the same vintage in Douro, Portugal. I even drank a bottle the awful night I'd killed Gala. It was my own choicest choice.

"Sir?" The orderly was waiting.

I looked at the bottle; then, at the orderly. My senses throbbed, stoked by yearslong privation. I indulged a brief daydream of murdering Smiker before ravaging the ribeye. And afterwards, I'd swig port over his corpse.

Smiker looked up from his paperwork to find his domestic and inmate frozen in place. "It's not a trick. Drink, eat. As much as you like."

I hesitated. But, eventually nodded at the orderly to pour. He filled the tin tumbler. "Will there be anything else, sir?"

"Cigarettes," I said, overtaken by the fuller dimensions of my long-suppressed appetites, "I want cigarettes."

"You can leave us, Victor," Smiker said. He produced a green pack of Eckstein No. 5s and a book of matches from his jacket's welt pocket and tossed them across the desk.

"Sir," the orderly said with a bow.

And soon thereafter flew the coop.

———

Despite overeating, I also drank up all the port. My belly was fit to burst. Warden Smiker, only occasionally reaching over to reclaim the odd cigarette, contented himself with watching me gluttonize and swill.

"So, tell me about this special clemency," I said. I was

full of more than food and drink. I was full of feeling; revitalized, renewed. I had tasted, in the food that free men eat, the freedom that they feel. "I'm quite interested in what you've got to say." Me, slipping into an old and familiar hauteur.

Smiker nodded and lit his cigarette, sucked in the world's slowest-ever drag. "You'll have to do a few things first. Trifles, you know. A formality. Then you're free to go."

"What things?"

"You must outrun a man who will hunt you through the forest, from just outside the penal colony border all the way to Lurcu's Fachwerkhaus."

I had a good chuckle at that. I'd never known the warden had a sense of humor. "A human foxhunt, eh? Sharable diversion for cannibals and country gentlemen?" I slapped my palm on the table. "Splendid idea! A splendid idea, warden. Absolute aces."

God, I felt grand. Kopke stirring my brain, still swirling on my tongue, working its boozy magic all the way down between my toes. I took my half-dozenth cigarette, tittering in fits and starts. I was swollen, and drunk, suffering only the deepmost contentment. Smoke lazily spilled blue-gray haze through my lips. I could have sat there, with that man I despised, for hours.

If there is a cardinal rule for inmates, it's vigilance. No convict ever won a prize letting down his guard.

Smiker did not break a smile. He narrowed his eyes, stonily assessing as he slow-spent his cigarette into his lungs. His silence became uncomfortable. And soon, unendurable. I began to wonder. While I'd thought this a friendly game of checkers, the warden had, perhaps, played me a mercenary round of chess.

"You're serious?"

"As a heart attack, Eckord. Should I finish?"

You know what a rhetorical question is, don't you?

"Additionally," Smiker continued, "you'll want to reach the Fachwerkhaus before the poison's overtaken your body."

Before that moment, he'd shown no emotion. But Smiker's now-quivering lips twisted into a sadistic grin. He nodded at my empty bottle. His body shook. He was either seizing or trying not to laugh.

"Vomit if you like," Smiker said, "the poison's in your blood now."

It was not satiety's pleasant lethargy I then felt. It was chance's grim inoculation. Smiker's grin broadened to see Fate eat me alive.

I gave my brain over to panic-driven equations of time and distance, quickly realizing the variables I needed to figure. "How far is Lurcu's House?" My voice steepened with dread.

"Two kilometers, as the crow flies," Smiker said. "You had two hours from the moment the first drop reached your heart."

I was shaking like a leaf. Where was there a wall clock? But of course there wouldn't be. Prisoners shouldn't know the consolation of time.

"You have—" Smiker pushed up his jacket sleeve and looked down at his wristwatch. "—a little more than an hour."

The odds did not favor calling his bluff. I leapt from my seat.

"Eckord, the antidote," Smiker said. "You should like to know, I'd imagine, where it is located."

Detained to calculate my survival, I said, "Where? Where, man? Where?!"

Smiker smashed his fists into his desktop so that the

wood shrieked and splintered. He spat out each word, eyes twitching like mad, tongue whipping and thrashing like a decapitated snake inside his mouth. "The antidote is in the Fachwerkhaus *keller*, the basement below Lurcu's House." He spoke epileptically, in the cadence of a Gatling gun. "Waiting next to your marital bed, set on the night table upon which you dashed your wife's skull; there! There waits your deliverance, your antidote, in the selfsame vehicle as that just poisoned your blood. I suggest you take if to the dregs if you want to guarantee a full dose. Bottoms up!"

"What do you mean, my marital bed?"

Smiker leapt to his feet with an animal howl, snarling and biting at the air, a rabid dog attacking hydrophobic apparitions. He danced and danced and violently danced, throwing wild haymakers while stomping his feet so hard I thought he'd break through the floor.

The Torture Hutch's light constricted in the encircling knot of a noose being drawn. Smiker's speech fell into sinister singsong, absent the lyrical logic of rhyme: "No more questions, no, ask none more. The poison blossoms in your heart. Run, little chicken, little chicken, do run. But ask no more questions, I've no answers at all."

He laughed as if to bloody his throat or vomit out his raving menace. The performative laughter of a lunatic. I was in a stageplay set for an asylum.

I ran. I ran away from his laughter and toward saving my life.

————

I KEPT A GOOD PACE, TOXIC BALLAST NOTWITHSTANDING.

Where my muscles might have otherwise quit, panic's limitless fuel did not fail to drive me.

It was not until halfway to the abandoned Fachwerkhaus that I saw the man by whom fate would have me hunted for game.

No. No, no, it simply couldn't be.

Hadn't he died, quite terribly, many years ago? Hadn't I sat beside Gala while she wept for him?

I'd attended his funeral, heard the bloodlustful big game hunters eulogize one of their own. Had even been pulled aside by that rosaceous Dutchman who'd gone rummy before the obsequies. Freek Holvast, brutal-ugly, neither face nor name so easily forgotten. Freek Holvast, who'd taken pains to relate to me every detail of Gala's father Walter's gory death in German East Africa. Trampled underfoot by a bush elephant whose rageful brain had swelled with musth. In my head I could still hear the weird Hollander recounting the attack:

"*De olifant kwam.* Walter made grab for his *pistool,* but *de olifant; snelheid, snelheid.* Speed! *De olifant* have speed. Much too much speed. He crush Walter. *De olifant* crush. *Verpulver de botten van de man.* How in English you say? Ah! Pulverize his bones."

Freek Holvast had detailed, in his half-Netherlandish pidgin, how Walter's bone fractures had punctured his pancaked legs, the stampeder savaging him through to his spine, disemboweling him; how jagged shards of Walter's own broken bones skewered his body's bloodied meat, nearly turning him to pulp; how Walter paled paper-white, blood gouting belly to boots, basting his field jacket and trousers in gore. Walter Borner died more terribly than most other men (even violently) did.

And yet here he was, now, before me; Walter, holding his elephant gun's barrel leveled to my head, steely, sharp eyes daggering into mine. Up on horseback, pointed tailward, he was strapped bridle and tether to his rider back-to-back. Trussed in crupper and hip straps, harnessed no differently than the horse on which he backwardly rode.

Outfitted as in his viewing day casket, Walter's black frock coat was now tattered, smeared with filth. Blow fly maggots wormed their way through buttonholes eaten through his funeral clothes. He was flattened below the waist, trousered legs like flags draped over the horse's hindquarters and croup.

It would be more accurate to say I breathed his name than said it: "Walter."

Words oozed out of his revenant's idiot lips:

"Tallyho, Eckord. Tallyho, my grim-faced friend. I see you there in the covert, my quarry. But I'm a thruster, old boy. Mark me, I'm a thruster. Mark me the very devil, I'm the thruster on your trail."

Neither his face nor his lips moved when he laughed. It was more a plague of laughter than the sound of it; a pervasion of the hearer's mind by hypnotic disease. It infected me, incubating a parasite madness, scoring psychical lesions over my brain. I was wracked by old terrors from childhood nightmares; razor-toothed hounds nipping at my heels, a frothing vagrant capturing me in a sack and throwing me into a dark and freezing river.

It was more than human fear I felt at seeing Walter. It was supernatural fright. As if witnessing the Pale Rider come with the Rapture.

Walter's horseman laughed, too, like a diseased, wild boar.

Their hysterical derangement stole my legs out from under me. Or, the poison was nearly done working its way to my heart. My blood felt hard and heavy, my feet fixed in place. My skin boiled with fever despite my breath showing as vapor in the frosted air.

I fell to my knees, my heart rabbiting, fingernails curling inwardly deep to cut and bloody both my palms. I was unmanned.

Walter and his rider quit their laughter; a terrible absence remained. I sensed the abyss, a vacuum, noiseless and terrible and underlaying all perception. There was, just then, not an echo of an echo, not a rumor's paltry ghost; no rustling breeze or birdsong, no paws crackling through thickets and brush. The forest was cold, and the air was iron-thick but voided. Empty, empty.

Then the woodlands' omens rushed back in all at once; this wild place, barren and deep as doom.

"Please, Walter," I said, "I didn't do anything to Gala." Exhaustion and dread had robbed me of the ability to believably deceive. I thoughtlessly asked that single question disclosing every liar's guilt: "Why would I lie?"

As cowards' self-serving pleas went, it was expectedly pathetic.

So there I was, a living man offered up to the dead on that dish the better the colder it is served, as delectable to Walter as my own just desserts. I fell on my knees, hands joined in supplication. "Walter, you know I loved your daughter." It might've been true, but I was desperately wheedling. "Can't you see that I mean what I say?"

Earnestness would have been out of place. Not that it mattered:

A vigilante couldn't hope for more than cornering an enemy turned belly-up and begging for mercy. And I was giving Walter that very gift.

Then, an added layer of unreality:

Gala's voice spoke through her father's mouth in a feat

of strange ventriloquy. I'll never forget the words. How could I, having heard them so often through our marriage's glass-smashing rows? Her timeworn warning, an enduring enigma, spoken as hauntingly as a war-widow's lament. Through Walter's body, my dead wife's voice said:

"For promises we'll only weep, if promises were meant to keep."

If I called it an existential shock, that wouldn't begin to cover it. Electric terror blew every fuse inside my brain. The world whirlpooled me inside its swamplike vortex. Hearing the voice of a ghost I created through the revenant hunting me for sport? Well, I must've been playing one card short of a full deck.

"Now get up and run."

Walter shot the ground at my feet, and I took to my heels. A coward's preference is ever for flight.

———

I DON'T KNOW IF I LOST WALTER AND HIS HORSEMAN DIVING off the promontory into the freezing river; I don't know if I lost them or they just let me go. I dragged myself out and away from that waterway, cold as ice, chills to my marrow by the river. With a premonition that death drew closer still.

I arrived to Lurcu's House at twilight's darker end.

The house was overlarge and half-timbered, its cruck's wooden blades raised toward the sky. Each of its five stories narrowed and engloomed at each story's greater height.

There was a widow's walk atop a spindly turret, tower and nest interposed between the house's highest point and the creosote-colored sky. Gala stood at the railing around the widow's walk, braced against an eighty-foot dive.

But was there still time to take the cure? All else could could wait to answer. Needs must when the Devil drives.

I ran into the house and down into the stony *keller*. The basement was densely dark and humid around the faint glow of a lonely candle. I followed its light like faintly whispered echoes, traced the icterine glimmer to my old night table and bed. Waiting on top of the night table was my bottled remedy. Already uncorked and breathing.

"Drink," Gala's voice whispered from the dark imposing on the candlelight.

"Gala?"

"Drink, Percival. Drink."

Percival.

In the colony, Eck or Eckord. Outside Lurcu's Gate, Percy to everyone I'd known. Only my mother and Gala ever used my whole Christian name.

"Drink, Percival."

What good would it do to interrogate the importunement of a ghost? I gripped the bottleneck and guzzled, swallowing one-quarter short a liter. Drained the port to its very last drop.

A blanket of liquid warmth tied tight around my body, the weight of unstoppable stupor dragging my eyes closed. My envenomation reversed, blood purifying through the bone-deep exhaustion of surviving too close a brush. An emptiness gnawed at my core, my mind spinning outside my body, consciousness swallowed in an ocean wave of totalizing sedation.

I fell into hypnotic currents, submerged under the insuperable tide of sleep, sinking, sinking, drifting deeper, deeper down. In a strange house, in a strange forest, but now tucked in the warm linens of my old, familiar bed.

If God was good, He would let me sleep until my sin and all worldly sensation was gone.

————

It was a dream. Or maybe...a vision.

A house-height man stood over me; his body, ancient, superhumanly thick. We stood on the arena floor of the Hippodrome since replaced by Madison Square Garden in 1890.

I was shackled head-to-toe. Manacles banded my ankles and wrists, thighs and waist, a bear trap of a belt about my ribs, leaden dog collar wrapped around my throat, my head clamped in a cast-iron crown.

"Are you ready for your freedom?" The giant had tooth-less gums, smacked liverish lips. In the wavering warble of centuries, he spoke in the cadence of a modern-day Methusaleh. Who'd tasted antiquity's airs, known the speechless ancestors of mankind. Ever aging but never growing nearer death. Or so I imagined. His breath sounded like an open blast valve pushing heated air into the envelope of a hot air balloon. Body of striated iron, hands doubtlessly powerful beyond measure.

I was a speck on the empty vastness of the Hippodrome floor, minuteness underscored by both my innumerable shackles and the gray-bearded sentinel whose shadow could swallow buildings whole. A superb vantage for perceiving my inconsequence.

The colossus persisted to ask me, "Are you ready for your freedom?"

I was not ready, no; in fact, I repudiated freedom. Yes, I repudiated it! I'd happily be shackled for as long as Marley's Ghost. My confinement was cold but nonetheless a cold comfort; the devil's luck never found an unfree man once freed; that was my fear, and that's what I told him.

The giant chuckled with the peculiarity of voice of outliving centuries since his birth. (My guess was he'd grown old before Christ was born.) Tragedy and triumph, they both inflected his laughter. He knew, I ventured, how much and how little was a hundred lived years.

He was not one to very badly hurt others, I ventured, but neither did I think he'd object to those who did. Determining whether the behemoth was good, or bad, or even adjudicable by the measure of men, seemed easier said than done.

He was something, I thought, greater (and more terrible) than Man.

Notions of morality were obscured by the fog of his origins, full of phantasms from long ago; an epoch of primitives cowering at lightning strikes, of ritualized compulsion, of infants lain atop sacrificial altars and savagery lain upon dead husbands' brides. Times of terribleness celebrated with glee, wonder equated to terror. His laughter was of a fickle demigod, its meaning confounding, unknown.

Having laughed to his satisfaction, the giant said, "But you're already made free."

I looked down, saw myself unshackled.

Raising back up, I found myself surrounded by resurrection, of every death I'd mourned before I'd been to prison; my parents and their friends, cousins and uncles and aunts, many unremembered for years, by bedridden intimates expired in the reign of Typhoid Mary, hometowners shrapneled in the skirmish of a small Cuban war.

All of them. All of the departed, anyone who ever meant something to me, whether I'd bothered to attend their funeral or just raised a glass to their memory. Dozens of souls risen from earth into present attendance.

And then, creeping like a rolling fog, the scoundrels came marching in. It was every grifter, hophead and goon I'd ever gone slumming with; the *maquereaux* who'd turned girls into supine human turnstiles, the gamblers who'd dissolved their daughters' dowries and wives' rainy day funds inside of mob-run policy shops; the confidence men tied to Tammany, the gamesmen who rooked upper-crust rubes; the morphinomaniacs who bedded in Chinese opium dens, the incurable inebriates who'd roamed beerhouse to dramshop, surrendering their last pennies before panhandling for more.

The Hippodrome's atmosphere turned to dark, my family and the other decent folk fading away while around me shadows swarmed. The remaining stragglers were those acquaintances I'd scraped from the bottom of the barrel; untrustworthy, erstwhile partners in vice. Here were the cretins itching to cuff a mouthy whore after a dustup with another pimp; here, the soul-empty bounders who roamed midnight's back alleys with jackknives; here, the syphilitics who'd infected starry-eyed farmgirls by whole busloads of rural disembarkation, then bragged to anyone who'd hear it at every low-rent saloon. These many villains I'd known, now become my audience, outnumbering the betters of my life by at least two to one.

And beyond the company of scum, I saw the giant retreat towards the light. The good folk decamped alongside him, following him like lodestar, disappearing toward their glowing beacon while my darkness closed in.

I tried to chase after those decent men and women I'd known in younger years; they were now leaving the arena, as many now going as had already gone. But I was barred by a barricade of hoodlums and predators, walled off by human animals; with sharp knives and sharper teeth, a chorus to sing the symphony of destruction. The wall of deadly sinners circled tight around me, each of them a blood-mortared brick bearing a sinister grin.

Behind them all, I saw Gala, now wretched and beautiless. She smiled over their phalanx, a corpse-witness to my comeuppance. Lips hung from her rotting face, though not rotted enough to hide her hideous smile.

It was then that I realized what I had drunk inside Lurcu's House was not the antidote. No, what I had drunk was, in fact, something to cure my wickedness from the earth.

My promises were never meant to keep.

BOXED BREAKFAST

I spooned out a pocket of diced bacon from under my Cobb salad's boiled yolk, staring out the diner's plate glass window at passersby. I was both a perennial voyeur of this city and one of its wildlife species. I'd lived here too long to go anywhere else. Big cities ruin you.

You have to realize, I had bona fides. As far as urban anthropology, I'd seen it all. The bag ladies one spinsterish deviation below me, the big-bellied sanitation workers crucifying stuffed animals on their garbage trucks' bullbars, coffee-swilling go-getters with starched collars and incipient twitches.

But this was something new.

He wore an improvised cassock made of burlap potato sacks, unevenly whip-stitched together and smeared with fungal grunge. A cliché-stamped Spanish cedar box sat where his head was supposed to be.

A box-head.

His shoeless feet kneaded the sidewalk's grit with soot-smeared toes, toenails uncut since dial-up and blacker than the soot that sullied them.

He pointed his knob-knuckled finger right at me, fingernail like the spine on a blackthorn sloe.

What have we here? A new species of nutter, then.

Well, the city's always belonged to schizoids and winos, main characters and whores, strays and thieves; the rest of us are but the workaday humps of temporary estate. The box-headed man was no sorer a thumb than, say, the neon-dreadlocked nudist who stood in refuse bins singing Parliament Funkadelic, or the chain-smoking Saigonese in his sheer kimono, the one who walked his leashed ocelot past my building every day.

That is to say, when I saw the box-head shaking his finger at me like a teacher's pointer, I waited for something more interesting to happen. And when nothing did, no dark prophecy fulfilled, no random acts of violence, I was diverted back to my plate. Flitch and yelk don't eat themselves.

But box-head's peculiar madness insisted upon my attention. Lunatics, you'd be surprised, are some of them strivers, too.

He broached my booth's window, the hinged panel sealing the front of his head's wooden box swinging open.

My jaw dropped at once with my spoonful of Cobb.

There was no head inside the box. Instead, a diorama. A hospital scene, with dollhouse-sized beds and teensy overbed tables, a trapeze bar little bigger than a toothpick, a sugar-cube-sized EKG; the miniatures of a serious hobbyist, to boot.

The hospital scene's players were glossy handmade ceramics, colored from irreality's gaudy palette; maraschino lips and fingertips, glow-green chemlight eyes and sterling silver skin. So lifelike I smelled their sickness, saw their eyes wetly glistening hopelessness.

But, was that…? No. But, yes. Yes, it was.

Dead-center of the diorama was me, uncannily captured in figurine form, holding a newborn baby with a humidor for a head.

Box-head pulled away from my window and slapped

shut his stage-set-face's open flap. Then he turned away. And he ran.

———

A VOLCANO IN MY SKULL SHOOK ME OUT OF SLEEP. A caustic dribble spilled from my ear holes to sting my quivering jowls. A noise, of thousands of dropped pots and pans, all clanging in my head.

It felt all wrong.

I dropped from my bed like dead weight and stumbled toward the toilet, reaching to open the mirrored medicine cabinet over the sink.

How could I have seen my reflection? I can't explain it. But, yes, even changed, I saw myself, saw with eyes I didn't have, saw my new self in the mirror:

Perfectly sanded. And very well-varnished.

FINDING ERLAND

I t was hard to see through two black eyes, harder still in the rain. Worse with her injured ankle, walking on the narrow dirt paths turned to mud. Around her, the domain of creaturedom concealed by the thousand hemlocks and beeches, the barreling thunder, the groaning trees. Wolves out there, maybe, a starving mountain lion, some other demented predator.

Stipp. He was out there, too.

The pain was in places she'd never felt pain before. A perforated eardrum, broken ribs, a torn eyelid, her senses dulled. The world smelled like pennies, every light was red, all noise a static snowfall of hostility's master frequency.

Stopping, so that her broken toes and contused knee and burning lungs quit throbbing, even for a second, just brought Stipp that much closer, that much faster.

The only relief was the rain, as cold as rain can be before snow. The icy torrents dampened the painful swelling on her face.

Something ahead, Delia could see it, if only barely; maybe a measure of human edifice, maybe the orange-yellow glow of a hearth. The light was kinetic, moved and swirled, wouldn't stay the same; the building (or, she hoped it was a building) morphed into other shapes and soon again was quickly changing. She limped toward those shadows now moving through the light. It was a cabin; someone's cabin, with someone inside.

She would've screamed for help, but the sting in her throat was interpreted by her brain as potentiating permanent damage; silence, a boiler's pressure relief valve. Delia fell under the shingled overhang onto the porch, her full weight smacking into the boards. The sound was of a dozen wet and heavy grocery bags thrown against the ground. That noise would bring them running.

No. No, after a minute (two, five, more) no one came. The rain softened. She'd ceased slogging under its icy lash; now her face was a heartbeat on fire. All her hurt was clarified and sharpened, the high-definition pain of aches and breaks, banging agony's drum in her meat and bones; it all came now she'd stopped moving. Had to get up, get up and get inside; a phone, or a gun, or something else, get something she was too fucked up to know she needed till she could could see and touch for herself.

It would require the same effort as lifting the front end of a car to get back on her feet. But she did. Because she knew she had to. She couldn't not get up.

Delia looked in the window, shapes liquid and dark and pushing out from inside the light in abscess-like fluctuance. But she saw, yes, saw a man standing there. Her throat hurt so bad she thought if she'd forgotten it ripped out, remainder sealed with stomach acid. Mute, now, and crying, the salt of her tears stinging lacerated eyelids, splits in her lip and the bites on her tongue.

"Help me, please," she finally managed, watching the man in the window as she swayed on her feet.

A figure, silhouetted, personless shadow, frozen in place; stood so still for a moment she thought he might be a left-over Spirit Halloween standee. But he blinked. Eyes the color of city sidewalks' dirty slush after snow, but as luminous as if all the world's streetlights were buried beneath.

Delia threw her hand up on the glass, streaking it salmon-pink with rainwatered-down blood.

The man didn't move an inch. Only leered with gray-glown eyes.

And walked away.

Delia slumped against the siding, fell, slid till her head dipped under the windowsill. She felt her body shutting down.

Then, the sound of a lock. No, of several locks turning.

She couldn't stand. Delia crawled, then, toward the door, yellow light spilling out onto the porch. The door, now opened; that, the extent of this stranger's kindness (or who knew what else). The palms of her hands, she felt, as they scraped the porch's wood boards, were on fire. Crawling over hot coals.

She made it past the threshold.

———

Inga heard the babies squalling and tumbling over one another in their travel crate inside the truck's camper shell. The smell riled them. Stoked their hunger. If she'd caught the scent, she knew the babies could catch it, too, and probably already had. Blood, spilled beyond physical sensation's proximity, transmitted remotely to her through the proxy of her kind.

The tail-turning bastard ought've known they'd pick it up, wherever the hell he caught the scent first. That shitheel had stretched child abandonment into psychological torture, so far as she was concerned.

His old man, too. Hell, it was the geezer who wanted to hightail it. With the *Ørblomst* in tow. Was it not nasty enough already to just cut and run?

Inga scented a female with him. Couldn't be more than twenty, thirty miles off. Probably inside of ten. Didn't matter. Across county lines, states' borders, through flood, fire, and rain. Hell, halfway across the world, and she'd still be hooked into Erland, tasting whatever he was tasting, wherever it was he was tasting it.

Smelling the same smell.

Erland, with a human female.

Inga clutched the steering wheel hard enough that the steel under the polyurethane grip squealed.

Done killing, he'd said. What the hell did that even mean? They were predators. Predators kill to eat. Foxes don't broker deals with the henhouse.

Inga couldn't playact his same self-righteousness. Mothers don't have the luxury of masquerading as reformed whores.

Erland and the old man's whole goddamn church-up, all that holier-than-thou horseshit about doing away with the old ways. Well, Inga liked the old ways. Those traditions had kept her children well-fed.

The men didn't deserve the *Ørblomst*. They were weak.

Inga would find them soon enough. This right now, this was just her on furlough.

THE GAS STATION MANAGER LET INGA PARK HER TRUCK overnight in the lot, such as it was: a big, bald patch of dirt in the middle of wild woodlands. "Hell, ain't no one ever comes out here anyhow," he'd said.

He waved to her just now. Inga waved back. He was friendly, but not in that obtrusive way where congeniality masks some darker urge. Genuine, she thought. She probably wouldn't eat him. Maybe not even if she were hungry.

There was value to human decency, she knew, even if it was impracticable for her (and even if the designation of "human" did not apply).

He walked with a drop foot and one of his hands bunched in on itself, she ventured Dupuytren's Contracture. Coveralls radiating a bouquet of stale urine, gas, and motor oil. Incontinence didn't put her off, animals pissed outside and liked the smell of their own piss. Boorishness was what Inga couldn't stand. But the pump jockey was perfectly well-mannered.

She didn't loathe people. Or, she didn't think she did. She did what she had to do, when she had to do it. Kids need eating, and mama's job to feed.

The pump jockey hobbled towards her truck.

"Shit." She rolled back the crank, sliding the window down halfway, hollering out her own greeting to preempt his. "Hey! Everything alright—" She narrowed in on the embroidered name badge sewn over his chest. "—Chet?"

Chet shook the hitch out of his giddyup and wheezed out a chuckle, juiced his limp and quickstepped closer so he didn't have to shout. He'd buried his good hand in one of his coverall pockets.

"Remind me your name again, wouldja?" Chet's smile, chipped and smoky-yellow.

She pursed her lips a little, smiling till her dimples showed. "Stacy. And you're Chet."

"Sure am." He yukked out his nerves while he tottered closer to her window. "I'm 'bout to turn in for the night. Jus' wanted to make sure you're holdin' up alright. Bein' out here by your lonesome. Not that it's my business what a grown woman does." Chet hesitated. He pulled two

Snickers bars out of his pocket with his good hand. "Got you these. If you're hungry."

Inga made an small show. "No, no, no. I can't take that, Chet. I'll be alright."

His face betrayed the genuine concern of someone with a sister he'd taken care of (or who'd taken care of him).

"Now you take these," Chet said more forcefully. "They's jus' candy bars, so you take 'em now. I ain't gonna be hurtin' for two piece o'chocolate." He rested his lame hand on the quarterlight and held the candy bars out with his functional appendage.

Inga touched Chet's gimpy paw with her one hand and took the candy bars with the other. "Fine. But I'm just going to have to bring you something sweet right back."

"Key lime pie, if you please."

"I'll hold you to it." She squeezed his crooked fingers and let go his gammy hand. "You're a kindhearted man. Some gal's lucky catch, I bet."

Chet blushed, looked away. "I'm the lucky one, I'd say."

A throbbing bassline in the conveyance of a roaring engine broke their sentimental moment.

Inga watched a Beemer wheel like hellfire around a nearby bend, EDM synth lines and kick drum thumping in 4/4 rhythm behind the tinted windows. The sedan whipped off the dirt road, riding dust clouds into the dinky station. Chet spun in time to see the Beemer park beside the pump. The driver honked his horn.

Chet cupped his hands in a bullhorn around his mouth. "Jus' closed up! Gotta pump her yourself."

The driver rolled down his window, pouring Eurotrash racket out two times louder than when the window was closed, then lowered the volume so they could hear him yell:

"It says full-service station!"

"Sure is," Chet hollered, "but I cashed out the register and locked up for the night. 'Fraid the pump's self-service till the A.M."

The guy kicked his Beemer's driver-side door open so hard that the torsion spring bounced the panel right back into him and knocked his ass down in his seat again. Firing off a volley of F-bombs, the driver worked himself out. Then, just stood there. Either leering at Inga or mad-dogging Chet. She couldn't tell which.

He wore a white Gucci sweater with the brand's telltale red-green stripe running vertically down the front. Blood spattered the white wool. Mr. Gucci swayed on his feet. He looked unhinged.

And was now making his way over.

"Christ." Chet shook his head, but he bucked up, went to meet Mr. Gucci halfway. "Sir, I cain't help you, I said, I'm closed up for the night."

As the men met a middle distance between her pickup truck and the pump, Inga detected a newly-familiar scent. It drifted to her off of Mr. Gucci's sweater; that same female blood Erland earlier broadcasted out.

Mr. Gucci showed Chet a picture on his phone; Chet shook his head at what he'd been shown. They did a little jawboning, a bit of dancing around. Amicable enough exchange. But when Mr. Gucci lipped a cigarette and went to light it, it changed the whole thing's tenor.

Inga was already striding toward them, a head taller than both of the two, when the pump jockey swiped at the douchebag's smoke. That set both men to screaming their heads off. Mr. Gucci faced his back toward Chet, hunching to light his cigarette while insulting and baiting the man. The douchebag saw Inga coming, waggled his eyebrows and gave her a shit-eating grin. Inga frowned how she did after stepping in a dog turd. Chet reached over Mr. Gucci's shoulder and, snatching the cigarette out his mouth, scratched up his whole cheek from under his chin.

Whereupon Mr. Gucci wheeled around and cracked Chet in the jaw.

It was a shattering haymaker. Chet was out cold before he hit the ground, where Mr. Gucci's cigarette rolled from inside Chet's good hand.

Inga smelled it clearer now she was closer to the sweater. Sensory data transmitted itself back to the kids, just that bitsy hint of blood driving up their crimson fever.

Mr. Gucci picked up his cigarette and put it back between his lips, then lit up and took a pull. He breathed heavy despite the barely-half-minute scuffle. Blood beaded a checkmarked cut on his cheek. Older scratches marked his hands and his neck. Tiny bruises, too. Defensive marks, that was Inga's best guess. She caught the paint thinner bite of chemically-cut cocaine seething from inside a fog of cologne. He was a type.

"Whose blood is that?" Inga had snuck up and got the jump on Mr. Gucci, two feet behind him before he had seen her.

"Holy shit. Would you check out this big mama," Mr. Gucci slimily cackled. "How 'bout I be the monkey, you be the monkey bars?"

Inga ignored him to look at an unconscious Chet. Then, looked back to Mr. Gucci. "I think you might've broken his jaw."

"Crippled cocksucker stole my loosie. Scratched me, too. Scratched my face. Little bitch scratched my face."

"Arbitrary violence is purposeless energy. More importantly, blood. Your violence wastes blood."

"Wastes…blood?"

"Blood is plentiful. But for that, no less precious. I might sooner waste gold."

"How can you waste gold?"

"You seem like you might be a little bit slow."

He flicked his cigarette and balled up his fists. "You big bitch, I'm gonna—"

"Doesn't matter. I can work with it." Inga sultrily smiled and winked at Mr. Gucci. She thus caused him, by her unsolicited flirtation, to completely short-circuit.

Inga turned heel towards her truck, took a few steps, then spun back facing the douchebag, eyeing him in expectation. "That's my camper right there," she said, nodding her head over towards her pickup. "You want to see inside?"

He cleared his throat and perked up like a dog who'd heard a cat. "You got something special for me?"

Inga winked at him. "You know I do."

The thing of it is this. Dogs may have a good time, but cats are much cleverer.

———

"*Det er en dårlig idé.*"

"She was going to die. What would you have me do?"

"*Uansett.* We no can save her." The old man's meerschaum pipe was too small for him, it looked like a lollipop stuck stick-first in his mouth.

"Anyway, it's done. It's done, and she's here." The younger one's thirty-six inseam dungarees rode up his shins the length of old-fashioned knickers. "I've let her in and that's it, then."

"*Så hva?* You send her somewheres away. *Ikke vår type.* On our own kind, we worry. Not on her." The old man cocked his chin out at the bruised and beaten woman lain unconscious on the couch. "*Utenforstående.*"

"Look at her. We're supposed to kick her out? When she's like that?"

"*Søvn! Jeg vil sove!* I am not care for *Utenforstående!*" The old man pushed off his stool. He went and opened the liquor cabinet, palmed a bottle of Atlungstad Aquavit and popped the cork out with his thumb. He hoisted the bottle, almost forgetting his pipe. "*Jævel!*" The pipe was spat out of his mouth at his swinging boot; tobacco embers shot like fireworks from the bowl. He punted his chair, watched it fly, shattering into splinters once it hit the far wall. "*Kuksugende jævel!*"

"Are you done?" The young man crossed his arms, watched his elder's nostrils quiver from the dumb rage in his blood. "Now you don't have a chair."

The old man grunted gut-deep and turned to look out the kitchen window, eyeing the trees' thousandfold peaked shadows filling up the forest dark. "We make rid of her. *Gi henne sparken.*"

"No."

"What 'no'?"

The young man stood up from the nook too small for them to comfortably eat in, with its too-small table and too-small wood-burning stove, octagonal percolator and skillet sitting on the range of what was, to them, a child-sized oven, windows and chairs all too tiny, too. He entered into the wider cabin.

The old man called after him: "*Hva tenker du på?* Where are you go now?"

"Getting the *Ørblomst*," came the reply a short ways down the hall, "just a piece. Just a small one to help her."

"You no do this! *Helligbrøde. Det er helligbrøde!*" The old man shouted. But he didn't chase. They'd already been running too long. He didn't have the will to fight the onslaught of youth and inexperience.

———

THROUGH HIS HORRIFICATION, THAT HUMAN MONUMENT TO douchebaggery told Inga his name was Stipp.

And Stipp served his purpose. Close, now. Inga knew she was close. And getting closer. Her offspring's senses were electrified with the amperage of youth. Despite their hunger, they too easily lifted the scent from Stipp's sweater.

Very close.

Though the drive was slow. And tracking, a painstaking process.

There were other things to scent beside the sweater. Whatever Stipp did to whoever he'd done it to, he hadn't tried to hide it. The shmuck had a grocery bag full of evidence in the trunk of his car; faintly urine-dribbled panties, lipstick with tuberculate rubbed off on the bullet, a dusting of dandruff inside the cap of a platinum-blonde wig, hoop earrings with sebum-smeared posts, strands of (real) hair coiled on the bristles of (what was presumably) the victim's comb. Inga understood better than most that predators had an overdeveloped sense of impunity, but it was a whole other thing to haul evidence of your crimes around with you while you drove.

Stipp obviously wasn't the brightest bulb on the Christmas tree.

For now, though, he had utility. So she periodically pulled over to untie him and let him use the bathroom, even hose him down and redress his wounds so that his meat wouldn't spoil.

Which slowed them down more.

Just then, Inga was pulled over on the berm of an embankment dam, in this zone halfway between sparse rurality and the desolate wilds. While the little ones tracked they passed their signal back to her, filling her senses as if she was with them on the trail. Fingernails ripped from fingers and meat scraped from nailbeds, bits of scalp attached to hair tangled in low-hung branches, bloody handprints left on tree bark and boulders, footprints set in dried mud.

And no rain the last two days. Give thanks for small mercies, she supposed.

Something tweaked her ears and nose. Something one of the little ones found. Inga slid out the cab of the truck, slamming the door shut behind her with her heel. One of the little ones came along presently, progressing by cantering knuckle-walk, halfway between a gorilla's fists pounding the ground and the gallop of an unshod horse.

Her little baby came out the clearing, fangs jut from its prognathous underbite, its lower jaw shaped like a sperm whale's mandible, holding something inside. Baby nickered, low and grumbly, and Inga smiled. The little one slowed its four-limbed knuckle-run to a crawl.

Inga clicked her tongue, speeding up her baby just a bit, come loping over with its apish limbs in a gangle. Closer in, it slowed its trot to stop in front of Inga, maw open wide, its offering inside.

A single silverish hair, there on baby's tongue. She pinched it between her fingers, put it up under her nose, snuffed at it. The parsnip scent of water hemlock. The old man's smell.

They weren't far off.

———

DELIA AWOKE RECUPERATING ON A PLAID COUCH INSIDE A stranger's house. Hurt something awful, still swollen, gouged, and fractured, but less unbearably than before. She was cocooned in athletic tape, bandages, gauze, alcohol and antiseptics sharp in the air. She'd been patched up.

"You're awake." The sugar-sweet tenor of the voice didn't match the man:

Gaunt, too tall. Delia thought his ash-blonde crop might touch the rafters; undershirt's armholes feeding a wingspan that overshot the ape index, knuckles gone down near to his knees. Pigeon-chested in the extreme with something like a skeletal fist pressing out from his breastbone; all overtop of distended birdcage ribs.

Even seated as he was on the wooden coffee table next to the couch, he was taller than a grown man. He smiled and Delia thought she saw teeth visibly shift inside his gums' sockets. His irises were the last shade of gray before white, and he smelled of fresh dirt and root vegetables.

"I'm Erland." He extended a freakishly large hand. "But you can call me Erl."

Delia gawped at seeing his elephantine meat hook. They pressed the flesh. She felt like a spider monkey shaking hands with a yeti. "Delia," she said.

Erland smiled, letting go his grip. He placed his giant paws palms-down on his knees, elbows oxbowed out. Was he aware of the wet plucking noise coming from inside his mouth? "You were very badly injured. I gave you some medicine."

"Are you a doctor?" she said.

"No. But then, you aren't a patient."

"No?"

"No." Erland leaned in with a smile describing either a sadistic deviant or a harmless prankster. "You're a trespasser."

A much older man entered the room, his stringy hair the silvering dark-gray of dirty mufflers, hanging past his wispy beard. The old man side-eyed Delia, obviously irritated that she was here, or alive, or awake, or all of the above. He gave off Erland's same scent, complemented by the robust addition of parsnips.

"*Få henne til å gå*," the senior said. He was built with Erland's same freakish proportions.

Erland spoke to but didn't face the old man. "Just a minute."

"Why you are here?" The old man stalked closer to Delia until she was brought under his shadow. If he had the temper he also had the size to push the roof off the cabin. "You are answer to my question. Why you are here?"

"I was running away."

"Running who?" The old man's lips clamped together, blanching the same pale bone-white as his ashy skin, wrinkles folding the corners of his mouth. He had gray eyes, too, but darker, and dense with speckled blood.

There was no world in which these two malformed creatures were anything but hideous, the old man being the more particularly repellant of the two. His flesh was a cartography of skin tags and shit-colored dysplastic moles, Bactrian humps where lipomas sought bodily escape.

His ugliness, however, was considered by her but shortly, as a voice began calling Delia from outside the cabin:

"Delia!" It was Stipp. "Delia, I'm here!"

———

Erland watched her back rack up ramrod-straight, face flushing red with the high heat of panic. He went and looked out of one of the cabin's front-facing windows. A naked man, his flesh riddled with bitemarks and puncture wounds, was out there waiting. An involuntary exhibitionist, knees-down in the dirt with a neck shackle clamped around his throat. The attached chain on the restraint let a good forty feet out, where it wrapped about a birch tree whose multiple trunks inosculated into each other in woody braids, branches appearing as bronchioles made out of knobbly bones.

Bragi shuffled in behind Erland. "*Hvem er det?*"

Erland's brows constricted while he made his inspection. "A naked man."

Bragi nudged further in toward the window to look for himself.

The shackled exhibitionist called out again, "Delia! Are you there?"

She covered her ears and fell back into the couch, slowly shaking her head and muttering sounds but not words.

"*Er han lenket fast?*"

Erland nodded yes. "Yeah. Around his neck." He pointed to the man outside. "See?"

"*Han vil henne såre.*"

Erland shook his head no. "Then why is he naked? And chained to a tree? If he really wanted to hurt her…"

Erland and Bragi looked at one another, synchronously attaining to the same sudden fear. In dreadful revelation, they jointly voiced their conclusion: "Inga."

Then they started locking the doors.

———

Tectonic footsteps made the cabin rattle and shake as the old man and Erland rushed back and forth battening down the hatches. They launched themselves to and from windows, rooms, doors; throwing bolts, slamming shut the inside shutters to the panes.

Delia went to the one yet-unshuttered front sill and peered past the porch into the wooded gloom.

She could see Stipp's muscle and fat in ragged bitemarks bigger than most animals' teeth, a masticated roadmap charting his skin. A glisteny yellow-white border of fascia and fat surrounded the dark-scarlet-pink of intrinsic muscle fibers. Whole chunks had been eaten out of his flesh.

Sun's last light spilled through merging canopies of birches, oaks, and maples. Night then seemingly swept the day from the sky all at once.

The air took on a sudden, sharp kerosene bite, draining into the cabin, smothering Delia from without. The chain to Stipp's neck shackle reclaimed its slack, an elongated limb working the chain tighter around the birch tree from inside the tree's shadow.

The old man brought a busker's soft-shell carrying case into the great room, stocked not with brass or woodwinds but instruments of more incendiary design. The metallic clanging of the rifle bag being dropped confirmed her suspicion.

She turned to look outside again.

A very tall, very nude woman emerged behind a tree other than that Stipp was chained to. She was not herself a beauty, but still beautiful; beautiful in the way, perhaps, of a satiated lioness sleeping untroubled in the shade while her cubs fed on her fresh kill. But also, grotesque; twilit eyes of alien tenebrosity, hair perfectly winter-white, her oblong breasts like remoras suckling her flanks, areolae pendulously swinging almost near her navel. She carried a shovel with the blade wrapped in rope and the rope set on fire. An improvised torch.

"Erl?" Delia said. "Erl, who's that woman?"

But Erland and his elder wouldn't slow their manic pace, busily barricading furniture against doors and shutters, their animal exchange shouted in their foreign tongue.

The naked woman stared straight at Delia; her eyes pierced Delia's flesh and tapped into her marrow, restrung her nerves and crawled deep into her spine; the woman's thoughts were slick and thirsty, slithering past Delia's eyes and thereinto her mind.

"*I brought him to you*," the voice echoed inside Delia's head, prompting her to press the heels of her hands into her eyes. "*I brought him to you so that you could see. We must bear witness the penalties visited each transgressor.*" Delia touched her nostrils dribbling wet and hot, saw her fingers come away with blood. "*If you let them shut me out, you won't be able to see.*"

Erland inadvertently hip-checked Delia while reaching to close the last shutter, shoving her hipbone-first into the sharp corner of a hutch, soft flesh scraped along the iliac crest. It sent shooting pains to steal her wind and collapse her to the floor. Her connection to the secret voice was severed by the jolt.

Erland slammed shut the final shutter, precluding from Delia her view outdoors.

"Here," Erland grabbed her hand and pulled her to her feet. "You see the brackets?" He pointed to Tetris-shaped steel fixtures interiorly mounted to the shutters.

A noise like muted bells being hit with hammers rang out in the great room. Delia jerked at the noise, twisted around to see the old man dropping a dozen pieces of squared metal stock next to the rifle bag.

Erland saw her see the stockpile. "Exactly," he said. "Put those—" Erland pointed at the steel bars on the floor, before grabbing and twisting Delia's body towards the shuttered window, slapping his hand by the brackets. "—into these. Got it?"

An alien night murmured through where the shutters' seams met. Whose voice had she heard? What had happened to Stipp?

Erland gave her shoulders a good shake. "Got it?" She nodded, though it felt like with someone else's head, her body distant from itself. Delia rushed the stockpile to take steel bars in each hand.

All three of them raced to load the bars inside the brackets. In no time at all, the cabin was secure.

They thought.

———

Inga ignited the kerosene circle she'd poured around the cabin. A stream of flames flickered then quickly grew.

Stipp threw his hands up to his face.

"Oh God. Please," he blubbered, "please don't burn me. Please don't burn me!"

Inga looked down at the torch as if she'd forgotten it was there. She laughed and threw it into the ring of fire. "Burn you? No, no, no. I'm not going to burn you."

Inga's babies had fenced Stipp in on the sly, hemming him up before he got the drop. They were more than three times as big as they'd been two days ago, a little bit bigger than very big dogs. Bullet-toothed malocclusions twisted their vaguely human faces, claws scratching their knuckling gait across the ground. Tiny, stiff breasts budded their convex chests.

"I want to go," Stipp said. "Please, please, I just want to go. I don't know nothing 'bout you. I don't know shit, lady. Swear to God. On God, lady, on God, on God. Can you let me go?" He shuffled on his knees, insensible, in a hysterical display, pathetic, making himself low, low at her feet, strands of drool unspooling from his mouth. "I need you to let me go."

"Let you go?" Inga's eyes like polished nickel sparkled facing the flames. Her overwide grin was full of sharp teeth that rooted themselves around her mouth. "That would be wasteful. You know, there are children, in some places, with not enough to eat."

Her hairless half-ape babies circularly stalked Stipp as they snapped their jaws in the air. One nickered, then two, then all of them; then louder, and louder still, growing unto cacophony, until the outrageous sound at last caused him to cover his ears. Louder and louder and louder, until his tympanic membranes came close to rupture, until the uproar was a jet engine firing in his ear canal. Stipp screamed his mouth wide open, pressed his palms against his ears and—

It stopped.

He pulled his away hands. He looked around. Only the dull static of crackling flames remained. Inga and her offspring were as immobile as cardboard cut-outs.

Somewhere inside the cabin, Stipp knew, Delia was standing there and watching him. He imagined she'd hoped to see him womanly weep, debase himself in drooling, idiot panic; if so, her hopes had been fulfilled. And the hope she'd see him die? "Delia," he softly said, not knowing why he wanted to call out to her. Stipp wanted her to see him, and especially to hear him. But fear had stolen his register.

"Do you remember what I told you," Inga said, leaning

in close enough for Stipp to smell caramel and nougat and milk chocolate on her breath, moist lips grazing against his ear as she softly whispered, "about violence?" He wept. Wept the tears of childhood's midnight terrors, of bed-wetting shame. Of God-shaped fear. "Violence must never be arbitrary." She breathed an almost sensuous air. "Do you remember why?"

"Please, please, please, please…"

Inga's fingernails protracted bony talons. Before Stipp could even flinch, she'd sliced through his nose. He gagged on his blood in a burbling shriek, choked through his amputated snout's hacked-open holes.

"Waste not, want not," she said.

Inga felt Stipp's blood absorbed into her flesh, felt its power build like fuel feeding an engine's fire. She again reached out through the dark.

———

"*I want you to listen*," the woman spoke into Delia's mind. "*I want you to listen while I do it. It can be for you, for us, for me, for my children. But it can be the very most for you. For you to hear. To see. To feel.*" Delia had lost her breath inside herself, her hand closing over her mouth. "*To kill this man that hurt you.*"

———

"Don't worry." As Inga spoke down to Stipp, her voice and face's shape became deformed. Razor wire consonants mangled her inflection, voice distorting deeper than a man's, vocal cords queerly clicking as caustic spittle dribbled from her lips. "The teeth of wild beasts can't hurt you when your consciousness is gone." She laughed the low-pitched pant-hooting of an ape.

Stipp squelched bloody sobs of hopeless resignation. Until he heard her beastlike laugh. Her laughter (if it could be called laughter) so distressed his hollow soul that it stopped him from crying. Worse still was when the babies laughed their own terrible laughter, too.

They sounded almost human. But only almost.

The first bite into his side was a species of pain he hadn't known existed. Stipp only stopped screaming when his trachea was eaten from his throat.

———

FIRE STILL RAGED ITS RING AROUND THE CABIN, EVEN HOURS later. Delia peeked past the warped bottom corners of the bathroom window's shutters. Those things outside, whatever they were, whatever that woman with them was, had grown fatter, and stronger, and longer, and taller, through devouring Stipp's portion.

The two men's odor of rooty damp earth suffused the cabin. Delia still hadn't learned the older one's name.

Dabbing her face with a wet washcloth, feeling the cold water relieving her swollen face, she heard Erland's footfalls echoing his patrol across the cabin. Back and forth he'd walked that beat since Stipp had been given to slaughter.

Delia left the toilet and went back to the great room. The old man was dozing on the couch, a bottle of some obscure brand of foreign liquor clenched in his knobby fingers. She came and sat down next to him. He roused himself and looked at her through a fog of alcoholic fatigue.

"Why is this happening? What is all this?" Delia said.

The old man was glassy-eyed, gone three sheets to the

wind. He had a mean and ugly face; perfectly fit, she thought, for a mean and ugly man. And drunk now, to boot.

Delia was surprised, then, when his face started to soften. Doubly so when he smiled and held his bottle out to her. She hesitated, but took it. Then waited. The old man nodded and so she drank. It tasted like it was made in a distillery owned by a Jewish pickler and Italian baker.

"I Bragi."

"I'm Delia," she said, hissing through the fruity spice. Delia handed back the booze.

Bragi took the bottle. He brought it back to his lips. But then stopped, staring at the label, before sighing and setting the booze on the floor. His arm was so long he didn't lean forward at all.

"*Det er en historie,*" he said. "I tell you."

Delia spotted Erland poorly concealing himself behind the corner edge of the hallway wall leading to the back. His face bore an inscrutable look. Masking the dread of an unknown future, the inescapable present; the resignation of knowing too much, or the anger of knowing nothing at all. And Erland turned away. Shortly, she heard him testing the barricades.

Bragi stared into the dim half-light the kitchen cast into the great room, air heavy with earth and smoke. "My people, I begin them. Before this begin time, but, I was man. Same as you woman. *Forstå?*"

Delia nodded. Though she wasn't sure she understood.

"I find *Ørblomst. Ørblomst,* this is thing name, thing for us. But first, thing is mine. Turn my life *lang. Lang, lang, lang,*" he said, stretching his arms out wide. "I living longest time. *Udødelig.* Always live. I cannot be dying. I am eating, so I cannot be dying. Always eat; always live. You know *ulv?*"

"Ulv?" Delia shook her head.

"*Ulv. Ulv, ulv. Ulv* are like this." Bragi's quiet lupine howl sounded just like mourning.

"A wolf," Delia said.

"*Ja, ja. Ulv, ulv.*" He jammed his thumb hard into his convex breastbone. "I am *ulv*. Be the same am *ulv*. I eat. *Kjøttet. Blodet. Blod, blod.*" Bragi held his neck out for Delia, pinching his jugular vein. "*Blod. Forstå?*"

Delia nodded again.

"I eat. Hungry. *Ulv*. I eat." His hands formed two carnivorous shadow puppets swallowing invisible prey. "Then I am from hearing *Ørblomst*. Is say to me. *Ørblomst* say, feed who are others." Bragi pantomimed giving food to someone else, that imaginary beneficiary eating. "Now are many *ulver*. We more *ulver*. We all eating, all hungry, always hungry, eating." His tongue gucked and slopped through him smacking his chops, shoveling his mouth full of invisible food. "*Mange av oss, mange av oss.* Eating, eating, eating."

Bragi touched a finger to his lips, then drew a half-moon to his forehead through the air. "We thinking then. *Alle sammen.* I smelling thing, many my *ulver* smell thing. I tasting thing, many my *ulver* taste." Bragi opened his hands with fingers splaycd, then clapped them both together. He shook them in a single fist. "We together. All together." His hands broke back apart. He touched his finger to his nose. "Together here." Then touched his mouth. "Together here." Then touched his heart. "Together here. *Forstå?*"

Delia could only stare at him. The thought came to her that she might rather relive the worst moments of her life than have to live any part of his.

———

A SHUFFLING OF EARTH AND ROCKS, OF DEBRIS PUSHED across a dirt underground, sounds under the floorboards. Bragi went stiffer than rigor mortis.

"Erland. *De er under gulvet!*"

Erland ran, rifle in hand, from the hall back to the great room, pulling back the bolt to chamber his Winchester 70. Delia jerked at its mechanical cold menace.

"*Få en rifle,*" Erland said to Bragi before turning to Delia. "You, too. Get a gun."

Bragi grabbed a pump-action Remington 870 out of the bag and racked the slide.

"Hurry up," Erland said.

Delia didn't know how to use a gun.

"Now!" Erland shouted at her.

She grabbed for whatever first thing she could grab from the bag and—

SLICE.

A bone razor shot up through a seam in the floor, separating a fingerprint-thin layer of skin from her right ring fingertip. Delia jumped away from the bag, a red rainbow arcing off of her hand, cut so quick she was too shocked to scream.

Bragi shot into the floorboards, opening a splintered cleft around where the bone razor sliced through. The retort of a half-dozen sharp claws shot up through the wood seams. The old man jumped up on the couch.

The air filled with percussive slits and snicks, a flesh-cutting chorus come dancing through the floor. Erland shot, worked the bolt, and then shot again, walking backward toward the couch.

Delia saw a long and knobby hand break through the shotgun-blasted hole. Each finger had a lengthwise spine feeding into a bone-razored fingertip, osseous talons over half a foot long. Bragi fired once, racked the slide, then blasted another round. A slop of gore and bone splinters exploded across the wood floor, the unseen devil roaring in pain, its monstrous tribe joining in violent complaint. Erland did a backward quick-spring up onto the couch and crowded in next to Bragi.

Below the boards the monsters went abruptly silent, leaving only a wuthering rustle too faint to pin down its place. Despite it, the two men aimed their firearms at every hiss and sigh, tracking moving targets that couldn't be seen.

A slithering and scraping worked the wood from below, noise like an armory of knives ceaselessly sharpening, all in one draw. Its noise doubled, trebled, then grew by exponents, until an army of scalpels was sharpening itself in the underbelly of the floor. It intensified into the roaring static of a signalless TV left at full volume. Uncountable claws shot up through the floorboards. One caught the rifle bag and dragged it to the far wall. Through her screams, Delia evacuated her bladder. She ran for the couch, reaching for Bragi as she ran, tensed herself to jump up into his arms, and then—

Bragi shoved her back down, sending Delia ass and elbows to the floor. She stared disbelievingly at the old man, who returned a bitter look of uncompromising survival. The noise belowground turned to a hush, even bloodthirst held in abeyance so that the monsters, too, could bear witness. Panicking, Delia shot right back to her feet, again to try to leap off the floor. This time she reached for Erland.

She almost didn't understand what happened. Not when Erland put his foot to her chest, not when he kicked out his leg. Only when Delia skidded backwards across the floor, sliding the same stretch over which the rifle bag was dragged to the wall, did she fully understand. Only when she saw Bragi's same merciless look now worn on Erland's face.

Her world turned on a dime. Noise veered in tortuous drips, motion a paralytic sludge, time turning hellcat-fast before rolling back syrup-slow, the ebb and flow of break-neck seizures. Gunshots continued firing into the ground, but they were seen and heard by Delia as if from behind soundproofed hurricane glass. Fever heat spread across her neck, jaw tightening, a fluttering equilibrium, the world an airplane cabin when the pressure starts to drop.

Delia found the voice (or it found her) again.

"See? Do you see now? How we're so easily disposed of. See the way they turn on you? What they'll do to save their own skin?" The tone was a selfless mother's plea to her homecoming daughter. *"See what it comes down to? It's us or it's them."* The voice turned to the same mother offering up a piece of poisoned cake.

In time's treacly drip, the claws raking the underside of the floor sounded more like someone slowly dragging a wooden boat over asphalt. The gunshots made the low rumble of earthquake aftershocks, muzzle flashes tree-sap-slow. Delia apprehended each time-dilated action and decel-erated sound, capturing interstices of movement too quick for her eyes to otherwise see.

There were holes enough shot through the floor for dozens of claws to reach through. Talons cut so close to the couch that Bragi and Erland jumped every time they sliced the skirt of their bulwark.

"They'll take and take, and give you nothing, and after you've gotten a little nothing more, they'll want to take what you don't even have."

Kismet. A happy accident in favor of the voice inside her head. Call it what you like. But when the men shouted and pointed at the rifle bag near the wall, at the fringe of the kill zone, to where she'd been given the literal boot—*they'll want to take what you don't even have*—Delia felt a rigid bit of bone petrify inside her beating heart. A bodily memorial to a hard truth already known:

Every man in her life would sooner hurt her than lend a hand.

Time resumed its pace. Worldly sensation came back to Delia at speed. Bragi and Erland screamed over the seething pit of overlong limbs clawing up from the broken boards. They begged her to throw the rifle bag full of ammunition.

That is not what Delia chose to do.

Delia walked to the closest window, beside the kitchen table, pressing her hands up under the steel beam that barricaded the window. The two men behind her screamed a thousand times no.

But she'd lifted it already, and folded away the shutters, and pushed up the window. She'd opened the gate for the barbarians to come pouring through.

Waiting for Delia, instead, was the unclothed woman. Tall enough to look right through the open window and directly into her eyes.

Delia wanted to say something clever, something edifying, something to mark her choice. *They're all yours, maybe*, or something like that. But she didn't.

The tall woman picked her up and set her down outside. And as the monsters broke over the open embrasure, she said to Delia:

"It's time for you to go."

———

Miles away, Delia could still smell the blood that had been spilled inside the cabin. She felt different, now. And hungrier, too.

PUBLICATION HISTORY

"The Tezcat Apparatus" first appeared in *Flash Phantoms*.
"Rats" first appeared in *Trembling With Fear*.
"Pujkamaunka Splash" first appeared in *Maudlin House*.
"A Woman of Distinction" first appeared in *The Gorko Gazette*.
"Odd Egg" first appeared in *The Genre Society*.
"The Golden Mile" first appeared in *Macabre Magazine*.
"In a New World, Its Basement" first appeared in *Roi Fainéant Press*.

———

The following stories are new to this volume:

"Infernal Tramps"
"A Vixenly Hexer"
"Meeting Ivor Voëlman"
"The EP™ Implant"
"The Black Gaucho of Revendication"
"Ever Shall They Feed"
"Eguisto Zanosi's Fast"
"If Promises Were Meant to Keep"
"Boxed Breakfast"
"Finding Erland"

ALSO BY ALEX GRASS

BLACK RIVER LANTERN

DRECK

A BOY'S HAMMER

ATTRIBUTION

The book design and interior artwork are both by the author, in some instances using images from the public domain. The credit for those public domain images reads as follows:

"H.E. Walter Electric Burglar Alarm" by Get Archive is in the Public Domain, CC0, and appears before the story "The Tezcat Apparatus" in this collection.

"Meyer Zeit-Vertreib 2 Tafel 083" by Wikimedia Commons is in the Public Domain, CC0, and appears before the story "Rats" in this collection.

"Netsuke of a Man and an Egg" from The Met Collection is in the Public Domain, CCo, and appears before the story "Odd Egg" in this collection.

"The Witches Sabbath" by Luis Ricardo Falero is in the Public Domain, CCo, and appears before the story "A Vixenly Hexer" in this collection.

"Hag Sculpture" by Wikimedia Commons is in the Public Domain, CCo, and appears before the story "Ever Shall They Feed" in this collection.

"A Group of Doctors Performing Surgery in a Hospital" by Jannes Jacobs is free to use under the Unsplash License, and appears before the story "The EP™ Implant" in this collection.

"Desatota Wild Horse Gather: Day Two" by Bureau of Land Managements Nevada in in the Public Domain, CCo, and appears before the story "The Black Gaucho of Revendication" in this collection.

AUTHOR STATEMENT AGAINST AI

This entire book (including every word of the text and every pixel of interior and exterior graphic design) was created without the use of generative AI. A draft of this book was run through Pangram AI-detection software and found to be **100% Human Written. I will never use AI to write or create art.** *

---

* PANGRAM REPORT AVAILABLE AT: *https://drive.google.com/file/d/1t_jV4ff8X0qfjp U059fkGFP8V6Xga7uu/view?usp=sharing*

www.ingramcontent.com/pod-product-compliance
Lightning Source LLC
Chambersburg PA
CBHW061422160726
47995CB00003B/710